East Londoner Derek Smith has written many plays and short stories for BBC TV and radio, as well as five children's books. His novel *Frances Fairweather – Demon Striker* (Faber, 1996) was shortlisted for The Children's Book Award. He holds story-writing workshops in schools and runs a creative writing course for adults at City University.

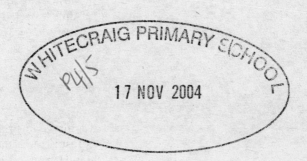

by the same author

HARD CASH
THE GOOD WOLF
THE MAGICAL WORLD OF LUCY-ANNE
FRANCES FAIRWEATHER – DEMON STRIKER

DEREK SMITH

Half a Bike

faber and faber

First published in 2001
by Faber and Faber Limited
3 Queen Square London WC1N 3AU
Published in the United States by Faber and Faber, Inc.,
an affiliate of Farrar, Straus and Giroux, New York

Photoset by Faber and Faber Ltd
Printed in England by Mackays of Chatham plc,
Chatham, Kent

© Derek Smith, 2001

The right of Derek Smith to be identified as author
of this work has been asserted in accordance with
Section 77 of the Copyright, Designs and Patents Act 1988

A CIP record for this book
is available from the British Library

ISBN 0–571–20713–8

2 4 6 8 10 9 7 5 3 1

Chapter 1

Roy looked at the wall in the small hallway, then stretched his arms along it. He couldn't quite reach. Would it fit? Was there room for a bike in this hall? His mother's voice drifted to him through the open front door. She was down the end of the path by the front gate. On the pavement was her piano and the two removal men standing with arms folded.

'Please,' she said plaintively.

'You didn't say it was on the first floor,' said one of the men.

'I'm on my own, you see,' she said.

Roy blocked out the voices. There was little he could do, except get told off for being in the way. Anyway, it was her piano. Having thought this he felt a bit mean. He liked her playing it and it had always been part of the flat. The old flat. All right, he wanted it in the new one and he wished they would get on with it because the longer it took the worse mood she would be in.

Moving was horrible. Even when he tried helping out – he always seemed to be in the way when the men were coming through with furniture. They shouted at him, and then Mum shouted at him. And all he was doing was moving boxes in like she asked him to.

The shouting had seemed to be going on for ever. Only a week really but what a long week. Packing everything into boxes while his mum got more and more upset. And here it all was – still in boxes. This was it. The new place.

So was the hall big enough? His mum had worried about the width of the stairs, whether there was room to turn the piano into the front room at the top. His worry was the hall. And it was simple enough. If he was going to get a bike then this is where it would have to be kept.

From his pocket he took out the tape measure. It was a metal tape with a spring. You pulled it out and then pressed down a clip to keep the tape out. He found it difficult to do by himself, but, by stretching his arms out and locking the tape, he was just about able to hold it against the wall. 163 centimetres plus the tape holder. Call it 170. How long was a bike?

The hall was wide enough. You came in the main door, then facing you at the end of the 170-centimetre-long hallway were two front doors. One for the woman downstairs and one for their flat. Would the lady downstairs say anything about a bike in the hallway? That is, if the hallway was long enough.

His mother came striding through.

'They're going to do it,' she said with obvious relief. 'But they've got to get some more help.'

'That's good,' said Roy.

'They've phoned on the mobile,' said his mother. 'And their mates are coming. I'm going to make them a cup of tea. Will you run round the corner and get some biscuits?'

He knew it wasn't a question. Not in her mood.

'Let's have the money,' he said.

She opened her purse and sighed. 'I don't know how we're going to manage this week. What with one thing and another. And I'll have to give them a tip.'

Roy didn't respond. The other day he dared to ask about the possibility of getting a bike when they moved – and got an earful. As if it was his fault they didn't have any money. She made it sound like it was. But if she didn't smoke . . . He'd worked it out. For the cost of twenty packets he could have a second-hand bike. But he knew she'd scream at him if he told her.

She gave him a pound. 'Now don't dawdle.' She indicated the removal men smoking at the front gate. 'I've got to keep in with them. Suppose they just left it there?'

'Back soon,' he said.

At the end of the path he had to go between the men, who were dressed in blue overalls. One of them, who had ginger hair and a moustache, said:

'Nice lady, your mum.'

For a second Roy didn't answer. It was difficult to think of his mum as nice. She was there. Sometimes she was all right and sometimes he hated her.

'Quite nice,' he said.

The man grinned. 'Good-looking.'

Roy felt embarrassed now. He certainly didn't think his mum was good-looking and was quite amazed this man did. Was he being teased?

'Hard being on her own though,' said the other man.

His mother's voice came to him from the front step. 'Stop bothering them, Roy. Just go and get some biscuits.'

He thought of saying 'It's not my fault. It's them,' but didn't. That would just get him a telling-off. If there was one thing he'd learnt it was that grown-ups don't like being told they're wrong. Even if they are.

So he said, 'Right,' and set off down the road.

Chapter 2

He knew there was a high street at the end of the road because they had come up along it on the way to the house. But other than that he didn't know where he was or where anything was. He felt rather afraid. He was on his own on a street he didn't know. All around him people he didn't know. If he took a wrong turning he might keep searching for ever. Going round and round and further and further away. He didn't like asking adults directions – and wouldn't if he could help it.

The houses on either side were large and semi-detached with a small garden in front. Quite a lot had been made into flats like his own. He wondered who lived in them all, what they did there. Did mums shout at kids, and dads do whatever dads did. He couldn't remember too much about dads. Drink beer and watch football, maybe.

A pity you can't see through brick. He would have liked to know just what other people were like. How they lived. But every house had curtains up. Every house was keeping its secrets.

The pavement was wide with trees every thirty metres or so. They had all been cut back, and with their oval crown of leaves they looked a bit like lollipops stuck in the ground. The wide pavement pleased him. You could ride a bike down that. Not that the road was busy. It had road humps – and that was good too. It slowed you up a bit but was lots safer. And if you were really speedy you could beat the cars.

The day was warm and he was grateful to be away from the house. To be away from all the moaning adults, to walk without anyone on his back telling him where to put his feet or to straighten up or get out the way. This road had some space.

Once all the moving was done with – it might be all right. Especially if he could get a bike . . .

A hundred and seventy centimetres, the hallway. It was probably long enough but you also had to think about the door opening. The main door opened inwards. It would swing round onto the bike. He couldn't use the other wall because of the meter cupboard – and anyway he couldn't put his bike in front of the lady downstairs' door. In front of your own door – well, you don't mind it being a bit awkward if it's your bike. But the main door when it swung – would it open far enough not to be a nuisance if a bike was there?

Of course there were hooks. He'd seen a picture in a bike magazine. Big hooks you screwed quite high on the wall, and hung the front wheel on them so the bike stood upright on its back wheel like a rearing horse. Except he wasn't sure how you put long hooks in – and he'd rather not have a go. It might really damage the wall.

Ahead was a boy cycling towards him on the pavement. He instantly saw from the flat handlebars that it was a mountain bike. And as it drew closer he saw it had centre-pull brakes and was shiny black.

As the boy drew up Roy called, 'Hey! Smart bike.'

The boy pulled his brakes and stopped just in front. He was a plumpish boy with heavy cheeks and a neat blue and white helmet. He wore black leather, fingerless gloves.

'Got it for my birthday,' said the boy.

Roy looked the bike over. The paintwork was shiny black and clean. The pedals and chain wheels gleamed silver in the sunlight. Roy came in closer and knelt down. He glanced up at the boy who had a pleased smile.

'Sure. Have a good look.'

The front wheel was quick-release and the tyres were pumped hard and had little wear. There were toe clips on the pedals. Roy raised himself to examine the handlebars. The grips were soft and spongy and by each one were thumb levers to work the gears and the chain wheels. Roy held the grips and then reached for the brakes. He pulled and the brakes instantly gripped.

'Solid,' said the boy.

Roy nodded and released the brakes. 'Bet it cost.'

'Two hundred and thirty pounds.'

Roy whistled.

'And £72 for the accessories,' said the boy.

Roy gasped and then said, 'What's that include?'

The boy numbered them off on his fingers. 'Helmet, pump, lights, lock, spanners, tyre levers and a chain tool. Oh yes, and a bike bag. We thought of getting panniers but then me and Dad didn't think we'd use them much.'

Roy wondered what the boy's dad did that he could spend that much. More money than Roy could ever think of. Hundreds. What did the boy say? Two hundred and something, and then seventy for accessories. The figures made him feel faint. Unthinkable money.

'Your dad must be rich.'

'I wouldn't say rich,' said the boy, 'but we just believe in getting the best.'

Roy knew that though the bike was good it was by no means the best. He'd read of bikes that cost thousands. Not that he'd ever seen one, though.

'If you buy cheap,' said the boy, 'you get rubbish.'

'Second-hand can be all right,' said Roy.

The boy screwed his nose up. 'Wouldn't touch second-hand. You don't know what greasy fingers have been on it.'

Roy knew he wouldn't say no to third-hand, fifth-hand, twentieth-hand. 'You can wipe finger marks off,' he said.

'Not the feel of 'em,' said the boy. He was leaning forward over the handlebars twisting the front wheel. 'Like my dad says. It comes down to standards. You pay rubbish you get rubbish.'

Roy had nothing to say. He knew in the boy's eyes he was in the rubbish market.

'I ain't seen you before,' said the boy.

'Just moving in,' said Roy. He pointed back up the road – and at the same time remembered what he was supposed to be doing. 'Gotta go – or me mum'll kill me.' He was about to head off when a last look at the boy's bike caused him to recall. 'Er – can I measure your bike?'

'What for?'

'For my hall,' said Roy. 'I need to know if a bike will fit.'

'You getting one, then?'

'Yeh.' Well he was.

'What sort?'

'Dunno yet.'

'How much can you afford?'

'About a hundred,' said Roy after a slight hesitation.

'You won't get much for that.'

Roy shrugged. 'So can I measure it?'

'Yeh.'

Roy got the tape out and with the boy's help ran it along the bike. '161 centimetres,' said Roy thoughtfully. 'I think it'll go.'

'I know someone who wants to sell a bike,' said the boy. 'Might suit you.'

'How much?'

'Sixty, seventy. It's just an old racer.'

'I'll think about it.'

'I'll tell him you're interested.'

'Yeh. Do that. Gotta go.'

'What's your number?'

'I'm at 82b. See you around.'

'Joe's me name.'

Roy was already running up the road. 'Mine's Roy.'

Chapter 3

For over a year he had been saying to himself, 'When we move I'll get a bike.' For a lot of the time it had been a vague thought, so far off that all he could imagine was the bike itself. And not how he would get it. But as the day of moving had come closer he could no longer avoid the thought. If he was to get a bike there *had to be* a way of getting it.

He had bought a raffle ticket whose second prize was a mountain bike. He wasn't interested in the first prize of a trip to Paris for two, and hoped he wouldn't win it. But he didn't win anything. He dreamt of finding a bike in the street. And then had to think up reasons why anyone would leave a bike. Perhaps it was a thief who had found a better bike, perhaps a boy had forgotten where he had left it. These thoughts made him uncomfortable as really the bike was someone else's, and, if he were honest, he should try to get it back to its owner. Better if a rich person would give him some money for saving his life. He didn't think this too likely but it had the advantage that it could happen any time.

His mother might buy him one. The two occasions that he had asked had got him yelled at. So he had tried to get his mum to give up smoking. And she did try. For three days she didn't smoke. And he watched her like anything, just to make sure she wasn't sneaking off for a quick one. In the end that caused another row. She couldn't stand being watched all the time. 'Like a kid!' she hollered. If she wanted to smoke she would. And she did.

He'd given up on Mum, and didn't think it likely that Dad would one day turn up with presents for everyone, including, of course, a bike for him. But that didn't stop him dreaming such things when he had his head under the bedclothes, and when that day a rich person hadn't turned up to be rescued. There would be a knock on the door and he and Mum would look at each other and say, 'Who's that?' And it would be Dad with his arms full and dragging something. The problem he had though was Dad's face. Did he have a moustache and a small beard? Or was he thinking of someone else? It was six yeas ago that he left, but that would make the present even better when it came.

If it came.

After the move, he had promised himself. Well this was the move, and if he wasn't going to spend all his life without a bike then this was the time. Look at that boy Joe. His dad had spent about £300. Imagine! It was enough to make you cry and kick. Joe had probably always had bikes; a new one every year. If anyone deserved to get it stolen it was Joe. And maybe Roy would. That beautiful black mountain bike. Joe's dad would just buy him another one. Centre-pull brakes, 21 gears – even toe clips. If Roy stole it he would have to get rid of them. In fact give it a paint job. Pity; that shiny black sang of freedom. But it sang too loud. If he stole it he would paint the bike some horrid colour, like pukey pink. It would still have the brakes and the gears (but no toe clips); the difference was that no one would recognise it. And also, no one would steal a pukey pink bike off him.

The high street had a lot of shops. One of the first he came to was a second-hand shop with furniture and boxes outside on the pavement and two bikes. They weren't up to much; one had a price of £55 on the saddle and the other £65. They were rubbish. One needed new tyres, new brake cables, a wheel was warped – and as for the saddle! Well you'd never be able to walk when you got off it. Rip-off.

He bought the biscuits in the supermarket. Mum didn't say what, so he bought what he liked, chocolate digestives. Great when you dipped them in tea and they went all melty. That took about two minutes. He didn't know what time he'd left but it felt a fair bit of time ago, and Mum would be waiting on the step angry. He began to run but was stopped by the bike shop. No one would expect him to speed past that. There were about twelve bikes outside in racks. The prices made him sick. Nothing less than £120 – and that one just looked tinny. Side-pull brakes – well you'd expect that, but when you looked close you could see the finishing wasn't good. And he bet the bolts and screws were cheap, and once they started to go then the bike would fall to bits on you.

He reluctantly left the bike shop, and forced himself not to look back. Over the other side of the road was a man on a racing bike stopped at the lights. He looked really old, maybe fifty or sixty, with a grey beard, but he wore shorts and had bare arms. His legs were stringy and knotted. The bike he rode was new and he was leaning forward over the handlebars as if he was in the Tour de France. When the lights changed he stood up in the saddle and pushed like crazy.

Roy shook his head. Why doesn't he just start in a lower gear? But the man was now in the traffic and cycling off at a fair speed. Roy considered for a little while the advantages of racing bikes over mountain bikes. Speed versus toughness. Now if *he* had £300 . . .

An ad in the newsagent's window caught his eye. 'Mountain bike, nearly new, £90 ONO.' What did ONO mean? Well for him it meant *Oh No – you can't afford it*. Then another ad, and this one made him take a big breath and sent a bolt of electricity through him. In that instant he knew he could wait for ever for his dad to show up or for the chance to rescue a rich man or win a raffle – but here was a real opportunity.

It was handwritten on a postcard and said: 'Paperboys or girls wanted. £14 per week. Enquire within.'

Roy knew he was going to go in. He knew he couldn't walk past as afraid as he was. He knew that notice said *Bike!* – and nothing else in his life did. But he was scared. He hated asking for things. You mostly didn't get them and often got told off into the bargain. Perhaps it was just an old ad and they had all their paperboys and papergirls. Except it was in good nick; the writing wasn't faded like some of the ads.

He had to go in. But what would he do if the man said no, you're too small, too stupid, too ugly, April Fool! But *Bike*, said the card, *in three weeks a cheap second-hand one, in three months* . . .

Twelve times 14 was . . . His head clicked away. 168. In three months he'd have £168. That's if he didn't spend any. Well, he could spend the £8, that wouldn't make much difference. He imagined £160 in five-pound notes. Crisp, new ones, flicking them as he walked into the bike shop. *I'd like to see that Peugeot Racer* . . .

A boy about his age went into the newsagent. Roy shivered. Suppose the boy got the last paper job? And he probably had a bike! Some people get everything. Oh, if only he wasn't so scared! There wasn't a dragon in the shop, only a man or a woman. And why should they laugh at him for just asking a question?

You! You want a paper round! Look everyone, look at this skinny kid – do you know what he just asked me? Say it again, kid. I haven't had a good laugh in weeks.

He couldn't go in. It didn't matter what 12 times 14 were. What mattered was the man in there who would eat him up. Roy walked slowly off. Perhaps his dad was somewhere, not far, even now thinking about a bike. Or there could be a rich man just round the corner on a horse just about to bolt . . . Or a pink flying pig with a bike in its mouth!

About to drop it on his head.

Roy turned and ran back to the shop. He swung through the door and went straight to the counter. Behind it stood a small Indian man with a tired face.

'You still want paperboys?' said Roy in a wavery voice.

'Yes,' said the man, his tongue rolling in his cheek as he looked Roy over. 'Got to be reliable.'

'Yes,' said Roy.

'You know the area?'

Roy nodded.

The man prodded the counter. 'Be here at 6.30 tomorrow morning.'

Outside the shop Roy was afire with excitement. Then, spotting the biscuits in his hand he sprinted back to the house.

Chapter 4

'Where have you been!'

She stood on the front doorstep, hair splayed over her forehead and shoulders, arms akimbo, face creased in anger. He knew that look and stopped a few metres away.

'You have been gone an *hour*. One hour getting a measly packet of biscuits.'

He looked down at his shoes. The heat of her anger scorched him. He shifted in his collar and blew.

'I got lost.'

'Don't give me that flannel!' She turned and went into the house.

Roy stayed where he was. He knew he couldn't go away but didn't want to go in. There would just be more telling-off.

After a few minutes he had made his way snail-like to the step. The main door was open and so was the flat door across the 1.7 metre hallway. Up the stairs he could hear heaving and heavy breathing. He glanced in; two men were sweating and grunting at one end of the piano, which they were trying to turn onto the landing. There were a couple at the other end he could hear complaining. Mum had to be ahead of them, trying to keep them off scratching the paint. So there was no point trying to get in. He couldn't get past them to do anything, and they didn't want him to help anyway.

He sat on the step, the chocolate biscuits still in his hands. He thought of taking one but knew it would be madness. He had sinned and if he took a reward for it she would never stop. Roy had learnt that his mother's anger always burnt out. The best thing was not to add to it. To say and do as little as possible. And to look guilty. That was essential. If he didn't then it was called insolence, and there was something she called 'dumb insolence' which could get you crucified twice over. No, it was simple enough, whatever you felt or thought, no matter whether you were right or wrong – look guilty. And, if you could, miserable too.

The sun had turned so it was just catching the step. He closed his eyes and faced it, and was filled by a warm orange glow. He smiled into the warmth and rubbed the sunlight into his eyes and cheeks. Behind him the grunting continued, with the occasional swear word.

In a little while all went quiet and he wondered what was going on. He listened but could only hear muted voices, and the odd laugh. Either they had got the piano in or were taking a break. He teased ants in the dust by his feet, made them climb over sticks and dry leaves until the men came down in a clumping of boots. Roy quickly got off the step, and four men came out stretching and breathing hard, followed by his mother.

'Oo-er, that was a weight 'n' a 'arf,' said one, twisting his shoulders.

'Please take this,' she said, and gave him a twenty-pound note. Roy gasped inwardly. All that money. She said she was going to give a tenner for a tip. So why twenty? He watched the man fold it and put it in his back pocket. For him it was just a tip on top of his wages, for Roy it was half a bike.

The men ambled down the path. His mother followed saying thank you so many times he felt embarrassed and stayed close to the house. Wasn't twenty quid enough of a thank you?

The men went to their van and his mother shut the front gate and returned to him.

'Thank heavens that's over,' she said wiping a wisp of hair off her forehead. She leaned against the porch and turned to him. 'You think twenty pounds was too much. Don't you?'

He shrugged. Of course it was, but it was gone now and it was his job to look guilty. And miserable.

She put an arm over his shoulder. 'Come on, let's have a cup of tea.'

Knowing it was over, leaning against her he went into the

house. Then up the stairs together like weary soldiers and into the sitting room. It was a wasteland of boxes and furniture. A cooker, a fridge, chairs, sideboards, cupboards, bits of beds, black plastic bags and dozens of cardboard boxes bulging with books and household utensils had been piled in the room as they had come out of the van. Only the piano seemed to be in its right place, against a wall in the corner, looking as if it never meant to move again.

They worked their way through and into the kitchen, which was a small room off the sitting room. Here his mother had set up a table and two chairs – the only furniture in it apart from the fitted cupboards, which were white and stained. On the table were tea-making things. His mother rinsed two cups under the tap and poured them both a cup of tea. Then she opened the biscuits.

'Sorry I shouted.'

"S'all right.'

'But you were a long time.'

He nodded.

'*Did* you get lost?'

'Well . . .' he began, then stopped himself. 'Not very.'

His mother grinned and crunched a chocolate biscuit. 'Well, we've moved.'

'Sort of,' he said.

'What do you mean, sort of?'

He gestured around him. 'There's so much to do. And then school and things . . .'

'I'm sure it's a nice school. And not for a month yet.'

He played with some biscuit crumbs. He just hoped it would be a nice school. For him. Then a thought hit him.

'I got a paper round. Starting tomorrow.'

'Good.' He could see she was preoccupied. 'I must go to the post office and cash my benefit. This is going to be such a tight week. I don't know anyone round here. Can't even borrow any money. So please don't ask me for anything. There's a good boy.'

15

He was well and truly warned off. And all that stuff to shift. Every box and bag would have to be moved and emptied. He was exhausted at the thought. His dad should be here. Then he said what perhaps should have stayed a thought.

'Will Dad know where we've moved?'

Her face went tight. 'He could find us if he wanted to.'

For a second he mused, feeling cold, then said, 'Why doesn't he want to?'

His mother sighed. 'How much can I tell you? How much do you want to know? I suppose you are old enough now. It's just . . .' She stopped in a sigh of thought, and ran a finger in the dust and sweat in the crease of her nose.

He watched her deciding, like a ticking bomb. Whether she would at last tell him.

'There's no easy way to say.' She pursed her lips. He could see a firmness setting in them – and then it came out. 'He's got another home. He's got another family.'

That came to him like a punch. He'd always thought of his father like a sailor on the high seas. Free, rolling from place to place. A week here, a week there. Until one day, when he'd travelled the world, he would return.

'How d'you know?'

'I've heard from time to time. And last month Jean saw him at the seaside. He had a woman with him, and two little kids. His.' She took out a cigarette and lit it. 'He asked her about you.'

'Why did he leave?'

His mother blew out smoke. 'I'd rather be shifting furniture than this.'

'Why did he?'

She inhaled deeply. 'He'd had enough of me.'

'And me?'

'No, me, lovey. He said I was too much for him. I caged him.'

'You had a lot of rows.'

'He was seeing her. I had a seven-year-old boy and was

depressed.' Her voice had gone dark and bitter. 'It was me who was caged. Completely. He wanted to go and come like a single man. Well, it was too late for that. He wanted a wife who would sparkle for him when he came home – and I couldn't. So he flew the nest.' She blew a smoke ring and watched it float slowly upwards. 'And now he's got another nest.' She smiled wryly. 'I wonder how long for.'

Roy felt small. He felt his father had left him behind like a bin bag abandoned in an empty house.

'We're better off without him.'

She put a finger under his chin and lifted it. Looking into his face and smiling she said, 'Don't go glum on me. I'm relying on you.'

He thought of his dad walking along the esplanade with two kids clutching buckets and spades. His dad holding the hands of a woman. But all their faces were blurred like in a bad photograph.

'Come on.' She went to the kitchen door and beckoned him. 'Let's shift furniture.'

Chapter 5

At first they just stood in the sitting room. There was so much. And all in one place it was so depressing. Spread around the old flat it didn't look so bad, but now the furniture, all heaped up, looked plain, ordinary, and what it was – second-hand. And in every space were all the boxes they had collected from the supermarket, stuffed full with the bits of their lives, and bulging bin bags like headless, very fat penguins. It was exhausting to look at and to think about what had to be done.

They started with the kitchen and moved the fridge in and turned it on. Then the cooker, which fitted into a space between the units. They connected the rubber hose at the back to the gas supply and turned on the tap on the pipe. Then Mother turned on the gas burners. They all lit.

'Hooray!' she shouted and slapped his hand. Then she did a little Red Indian dance whooping away.

'You're crazy,' he said.

'Fire,' she said in a slow deep voice, 'he come from the great God – and we give thanks.'

She looked at his serious face and stopped. 'If we don't laugh we'll cry.'

He nodded and gave half a smile.

'Let's get all the boxes that belong in the kitchen in here. Then we'll have room to see what's what in the sitting room.'

Having done the kitchen they put rugs down in the two bedrooms. This caused a lot of to-ing and fro-ing. Rugs were tried in one room where they were too small or too large, then into the other room they went, and back to the first where they would just have to do. Too-big ones were folded under and the too-small couldn't be helped. Mum said she would paint the floor space some time.

Then they moved the beds and set them up in the bedrooms. They spent forty minutes looking for bolts for his bed, his mother getting angry and upset as she went through the boxes.

'I know I packed them,' she declared over and over. 'I'm sure I did.'

As time went by she became less sure and more upset.

'Bloody moving!' she screamed, kicking a box.

She kicked and swore and raved. Roy kept well out of the way, keeping silent, knowing suggestions would not be welcome – until at last she sat down in an exhausted bundle and began to cry.

He let her cry out. And when the loud wails had become mute sobs he said, 'Couldn't we use string?'

She nodded weakly and so he found some. Then they went into his room. Turning the bed over to put the string through the holes they found the bolts. They were in a bag taped to the bed base.

His mother gave a laugh of hysteria, and they assembled the bed.

When they had done both beds they moved her wardrobe and his sideboard into the bedrooms. Getting hers up the stairs she was growing angrier and angrier as he became wearier.

'Don't you know your left from your right yet? Up means up. Don't drop it on my fingers. Hold it like this. Turn it. No, not like that. Oh honestly – can't you do a simple thing properly!'

At last they both stopped and she made a cup of tea. While they drank it she said sorry over and over.

'I'm terrible to be with,' she said. 'I'm sorry to take it all out on you. I know it's not fair. Just don't take any notice. You can see how it is.'

She was feeling better now. There was some order about the flat. Things were in the right rooms at least, and the place looked possible.

'I'd better do some shopping,' she said. 'We can't just eat biscuits. You straighten your room up.'

She went out with a bag and he went to his room where he flopped on the bed and stared up at the ceiling. In a little while he turned over and propped himself on his elbows. From there he drew himself to a sitting position, and turned to the window, which was about midway down his bed.

Directly outside and about half a metre below the window was a flat black roof. He could get on to it easily, Roy thought. He could read on it, get away from *her*. You could probably fix a bike on it. Yes – if the tools were on the windowsill and the bike was upside-down balancing on its handlebars and saddle. If he knelt down there wouldn't be much chance of falling off the roof. But of course his mother would go nuts. There was not the remotest chance she would let him put even a toe on the roof let alone a bike.

But she was out now.

The window was quite stiff and kept sticking as he pushed it up. Eventually he got it high enough. A warm breeze blew in the room. The sun had gone round the side of the house; it lit up the end of the garden but the roof was in shade. It was still pleasantly warm.

He climbed over the sill and onto the roof. It was so easy. He was suddenly aware of faint strains of music from underneath. Of course there was a room below. He'd not yet seen the lady downstairs. She had the garden. He would have to walk slow and easy or she might hear him. It was unlikely he'd ever be able to work out here on a bike then. It was the way it went. You had this brilliant idea – and then the real world came into it – and gave you twenty reasons why it wasn't so brilliant.

He went down on all fours and crawled along the roof to the edge by the garden. The lady downstairs' garden was a surprise. He hadn't been able to see it at all from the window because the roof was in the way. It was extremely tidy with a very green lawn, the grass so short it could have been shaved with a razor, and flowerbeds full of blazing colour. The sort of garden you couldn't do anything in without being shouted at. You certainly couldn't throw anything because it might land in the flowers; you couldn't run because you would damage the lawn. There wasn't a lot you could do, except look.

He hadn't even met the woman downstairs but already he didn't like her. Maybe it wasn't her fault for living under his roof (he already thought of it as his) but she did, and the garden – that was definitely her fault. Anyone who made a garden like that would not want children in it. He looked down onto her patio – there were a lot of hanging baskets coming off the house and fence – all popping with reds, yellows and blues, and pots of this-and-that dotted round.

Compared to that the garden next door was refreshing. The bit near the house was quite shady with trees and bushes and a few flowers, and then it was just vegetables. They were in straight rows. He could make out lettuces and peas, and other things he didn't recognise. Then cabbages. Then more thingamabobs and at the end a row of bean poles covered in green foliage and small red flowers all over it.

He could understand people growing food. That made sense to him. It must be really great to eat something you've grown yourself. It was then that a figure rose amongst the greenery of the vegetable garden. It was wearing blue bib overalls and had its back to him. A white-haired head followed it and then a hand holding a trowel appeared.

Roy backed down the roof, and by the time the old man turned round he was in his room once more.

Chapter 6

The alarm rang and for a few seconds he didn't know where he was. The shapes of things around him were unfamiliar in the weak sunlight spilling on his bed. The window was odd, and the walls a funny colour and empty. Then it hit him; of course, he'd moved.

And the paper round! He started this morning. He looked at the clock. Six-fifteen. Normally he would have tucked his head under the blankets and in half-dream half-story be the hero in his bike dreams. But this was no dream. Six-fifteen and no bike. And no bike unless he got up and did the paper round for four weeks minimum.

He threw the blankets off and quickly dressed. He sorted through a black bag to find clean socks and came across his bone spanner. With a yelp of joy he seized it out of the bag and held it before him as if it were a jewelled bracelet. He loved the shape of it, the feel of it. Each end of his bone spanner fitted five different sizes of nut. It was the perfect tool for his adventures – small but no matter what fell off your bike the bone spanner would save you.

But more than that. For this was his lucky one. The magic one that granted wishes. Grasp it tight, close your eyes and wish. It was the same wish daily – except today he wasn't banking on the wish. He was starting a paper round, and in four weeks . . . Magic bone spanner or not.

He put the spanner in his pocket and yawned. Bed looked so inviting but he turned away and quietly left his room. The sitting room was straighter now. The furniture was in place. There were still boxes and bags around but they were at the edges; there were no curtains yet. It was a room that could go either way. Like a film wound backwards it could reverse itself and everything go back in the furniture van. Or the shelves could fill, the curtains go up, the clock and knick-knacks go on the mantelpiece, and things of every day just get left around so that you knew people lived here – and weren't just dumping things on their way to somewhere else.

In the kitchen Roy had a glass of juice. He thought briefly about washing and then stopped thinking about it. Grabbing his coat he went quietly, so as not to wake his mother, out of the house.

There was no one about and it was chilly. He buttoned up. And might have enjoyed the feeling of having the world to himself but there was the paper round ahead. He'd never done one before and had lied about knowing the area. He put his hand in his pocket and gripped the bone spanner.

'Make it all right,' he whispered. 'Make it go OK.'

A man on the other side of the street was coming his way. He was walking quickly and looked very unhappy. Perhaps he was just unhappy at having to get up when he'd rather have stayed in bed, or perhaps he and Roy were the only two people left in the world. In the night a spaceship had come along and like a great vacuum cleaner sucked everyone in. Roy had been saved by his bone spanner. Maybe the man had one too.

In the high street he found other people alive. A few of them were waiting hopefully at a bus stop, and a handful of cars drifted by. The bike shop was shuttered, and there was of course nothing out on the pavement. The only shop open was the newsagent's.

All its lights were on, even though it was hardly necessary, as it was definitely day now. But then the lights made it inviting on this street of closed shops. It really was the only place to go. Roy hesitated outside. There were a few people inside and the racks were packed with newspapers and magazines. He glanced at the notice board, then stopped himself. Once he started reading it would be hard to bring himself back to what he had to do.

He gripped the bone spanner. 'Make it go right.'

He thought of the lie he had told. When he said he knew the area. A shot of terror twisted in his guts. The man could send him anywhere! He could reel off a stream of streets. *Do these – and be back in half an hour.*

He saw himself wandering the streets with a bag of newspapers, afraid to ask where so-and-so street was, and getting later and later. He saw himself coming back to the shop with a bag still full of newspapers and saying, 'Sorry, mister – I couldn't find the roads.'

The newsagent had come to the front window and was placing a pile of magazines. He looked up, saw Roy and beckoned him in. As if pulled by a string Roy came. Past the row of papers and magazines, past the sweets to the counter where there were two other boys putting on large bags stuffed with papers.

'Don't hang about outside,' said the man. 'People want their newspapers early. To read with breakfast. So the sooner you go the better. You understand me?'

Roy nodded.

The man smiled. 'I'm Mr Patel. This is my shop. And you are . . .?'

'Roy.'

'Glad you can get up early, Roy. Can you read?'

This question surprised Roy and he must have shown it even though he nodded.

'I had one boy,' said Mr Patel shaking his head, 'who put every paper in the wrong house. Chaos!'

The newsagent broke off to deal with a customer who seemed like a member of the walking dead. Bleary-eyed, head bowed, he mumbled something and handed over the money.

Mr Patel returned to him. 'What's your phone number?'

'I haven't got one,' said Roy. 'We just moved in.'

'Give me your address then.'

Roy gave it and Mr Patel wrote it down. He said, 'I don't want to have to use this. We come and get you once if you don't come in. Then that's the end. You understand me?'

Roy nodded.

'And if you've just moved in you don't know the area – do you?'

Roy nodded again, with some relief at being found out.

'OK – I'll give you a chance. I'll send you out with Ringer. He'll show you. OK, Ringer – show Roy how to do it.'

Ringer was standing at the counter adjusting the newspapers in his bag. He was thin with long arms and ears that stuck out. He nodded and sniffed.

Mr Patel handed over the bag of newspapers. 'You do Earlham and Clova . . .'

Roy took them. Ringer indicated the door with a nod of his head.

'Let's go.'

Roy followed him out the shop.

Outside Roy walked alongside. Ringer had a bouncy walk as if he could do it all day.

'He's all right is Mr Patel. Just make sure he don't lumber you with Hampton. That's two rounds really. By rights he should split it.'

Roy said, 'What did you say your name was?' Although he had heard it twice he wasn't sure he had. It just didn't sound like a name.

'Ringer,' said the boy. 'My real name is Paul Bell. Get it? Paul like pull. Paul Bell. My dad's joke. Not much of a joke, is it? But I like it. Paul is ordinary. And everyone else has got ordinary names like Dave or John or Bill. But I'm Ringer. And don't worry – I've heard every joke you can think of. There's me Uncle Ted who always pulls one of me arms and then pushes me nose. He thinks he's so funny. Still he generally gives me a fiver. This way.'

Ringer directed Roy round a corner. They continued walking.

Roy said, 'I've never done it before.'

Ringer shrugged. 'It's not difficult. Mr Patel gets up at half-past four and he marks up all the papers and puts them in rounds. You just have to poke them through letterboxes. He don't make many mistakes. Here we are.'

They were at a corner.

'We can share the rounds.' He took some papers out of his bag. 'You do that side, I'll do this. See where he's marked the numbers? Always look at the next –'cos sometimes they get two or three. They're quite well off round here.'

In the next hour they did half a dozen streets. All the papers were marked up so it was easy enough to see where they went. Ringer though was much faster. Now he was working, his pace had changed and had become a rapid stride. He rolled up the papers between houses and had no trouble with letterboxes. Whereas Roy fumbled with papers and letterboxes. At one house a snarl below the box made him jump out of his skin. Afraid for his fingers he left the papers dangling in the box and belted off with the growl in his wake.

Ringer waited every so often, then gave Roy more papers and his instructions and off they went down the road on opposite sides. Try as he might, Roy couldn't stay level with Ringer, who was like a machine perfectly made for delivering papers. He knew when to skip over a fence, never had trouble with a gate and never had to re-roll a bundle or take the papers out of the letterbox and try again.

After several streets Roy felt his lack of breakfast, but always ahead of him, across the street, was the scurrying back of Ringer. Up and down the paths, doing three to every two of his. Then Ringer was done and came back to help Roy. They did the last side together.

'Is it always like that?' said Roy with relief at finishing.

'Nah. Sometimes it's raining or snowing. Or both. Cuppa tea?'

'I haven't got any money.'

"S'all right. It's me uncle's. Does a great slice of fried bread. Come on.'

Chapter 7

'Two fried slices and a cup of tea – twice!' called Ringer over the counter.

The café smelt of fried fat, vinegar and tomato sauce. Workmen were at plastic-topped tables eating plates of egg, sausage and chips with large mugs of tea.

'Bit late this morning, Ringer,' said Uncle. He was short and thick-set, as if he'd been squashed to thicken out his arms and body. His head was round and red, and he had two reefs of hair around a bald lagoon. He wore a white apron with a bib and his massive arms were bare.

'Bin helping me new mate,' said Ringer indicating Roy beside him.

'How d'you do,' said Uncle as he made two large teas. 'Any mate of Ringer's is a mate of mine. Take your teas and sit down, boys. Fried bread'll be a minute.'

'Ta, Uncle.'

'Thanks,' said Roy.

They sat down by a steamed-up window opposite each other and warmed their hands round the mugs.

'He's me mum's brother,' said Ringer. 'Always been good to us, especially since me dad went inside.'

'Inside where?'

'Nick. My dad robbed a bank with a shotgun,' he said as if he were talking about the weather. 'Told 'em all to get down on the floor or he'd blow their heads off . . . Dad got ten years.' He shrugged as if it was some tiny event in a complicated life. 'That was over four years ago. Mum divorced him but still goes to see him. I don't know what to think about him. I've been twice. Don't like going. I think he was stupid. A shotgun in a bank! The whole world would be out after him, wouldn't they?'

27

Roy was somewhat overpowered by the thought of this boy opposite him with a father who held up banks.

'Did he shoot anyone?' he asked tentatively.

Ringer shrugged. 'No, and says he wouldn't. But then the gun was loaded and he could've easily. I mean what would he have done if a customer hadn't got down on the floor?'

'Maybe fired at the wall,' suggested Roy.

'And if someone had gone for him when he was leaving the bank . . .? It's easy to say you'd never shoot anyone but everyone in that bank thought he would. And so did the judge and jury.'

'How did he get caught?'

'A tip-off. Two days later. Dad says if he ever finds that grass he'll wish he'd been shot.'

The fried bread came over. The plates looked fragile in Uncle's huge hands.

'Ta, Uncle.'

'Tell your mum I'll be over at the weekend.' He turned away, his wide back like a door, and waddled off to the counter like a sailor on a rocking ship.

'We just moved,' said Roy.

'Who's we?'

'Me and my mum.'

'Ain't your dad around?'

'No.' After a pause Roy added, 'He's got another family.' He was surprised at admitting this but then Ringer had made it easy by telling him about his own dad being in jail.

'You met 'em?' asked Ringer, pushing the bread into his face as if it were a saw. The bread just seemed to disappear; whereas Roy had barely taken a bite out of his first slice Ringer was already working on the second.

'Just heard – that's all,' said Roy uncomfortably. 'Not from him. He just left one day. We thought he was at work but he didn't come back. Mum says he couldn't stand being trapped.'

'Well he should've stood it,' snapped Ringer. 'You're his, ain't you?'

'Yeh.'

'Well then.' The second slice had disappeared. 'Don't think much of him.'

Roy was lost in a tunnel of feeling. For a dad that had walked out on them.

'Sometimes I hate him,' he said. 'And sometimes . . .' His hair prickled at his neck. 'I dunno.'

'Yeh,' said Ringer. 'I know what you mean. Whatever he's done he's still your dad. I mean, you only have one, don't you?'

They both became silent. The two boys looking a little in the distance and imagining what might have been or what could be. Or what couldn't. Roy ate automatically, hardly noticing until the second slice of bread had a strange effect on his guts. He suddenly felt very loose.

'Where's the loo?' he hissed to Ringer.

'Ask Uncle.'

Roy went to the kitchen and poked his head in. Uncle was by the stove turning over burgers.

'Can I use the loo?'

'Sure. In the back room.'

Roy strode through the kitchen into the back room. There he opened the first door he saw. It was a cupboard, full at the bottom with cleaning stuff, but from halfway up were shelves of tools. In spite of his urgency he couldn't help looking. A long-armed tool caught his eye . . . No, no – it would have to wait.

The door next to it was the loo, and Roy greeted it with relief.

When he came out he washed his hands in a small sink, wiped them and, when he was about to leave, saw he had left the cupboard door open. He went to close it and was again caught by the tool. The others he was familiar with – the screwdrivers, the hammers, chisels, files, planes, pliers – but this one, with long arms and a strange snub nose, he had never seen before.

Roy took it out.

He held it against his shoulder. It came down below his wrist. At the lower end was a joint almost like an elbow. It had a feeling of strength and engineering. He wondered what it was for.

'Bolt-cutters,' came Uncle's voice from behind. 'Beautiful tool, eh? For cutting thick wire or chain. The long handles and those joints give you a lot of force. I had some fence work at home. They cut through the chain like it was cheese.'

'Nice feel.'

'That's a real tool. Made for the job, made to last,' said Uncle going back into the kitchen.

For Roy there was a sort of magic in it. What it could do, what it could help you do. His dad had had a box of tools . . .

Roy put the bolt-cutters back and closed the cupboard door.

When he got back to the café Ringer said, 'I've asked Uncle to sing.'

Roy looked across at the big man on the other side of the counter furiously buttering bread.

'What, sing? Here?'

'You wait.'

Roy didn't know whether this was a tease or not. From Ringer's face it didn't look like one, but you never knew. It could just be a trick that only you didn't know about. The one they always tried on the new boy.

'What does he sing?'

'You'll see.'

Roy could see he wasn't going to get any more out of Ringer so he left it. And went back to eating. He was still hungry after the morning's effort. The fried bread was nearly cold but still tasty.

Uncle came out with a trayful. He bustled around the café dropping plates off here, a cup of tea there. The speed's in the family, thought Roy, watching the performance; further impressed by the fact that Uncle knew everyone's name. Tea, John. Bacon, egg and beans, Bill. Two slices, Mac.

Uncle then stepped back against the counter. He placed his

empty tray on it, took a deep breath, and addressed the café.

'Ladies and gentlemen . . .'

In the brief pause Roy noted there were no ladies, but the men present all looked over in expectation.

Uncle took a huge breath, pumping up his chest. He seemed to be looking way above everyone's head. Then he launched straight into song.

The richness of his voice was a surprise. The song was in Italian, so Roy couldn't understand a word – but he knew it was a love song because of the feeling expressed by Uncle. Here, among the saucepots, the vinegar and beans, he heard the pain of a breaking heart. The man in the white overalls was telling everything – and it was impossible not to listen. It was not like a radio you could ignore, not like that at all, because the man was there – and he was telling everyone how it was.

There was not a murmur in the café. Not a paper rustled, not a fork lifted. The tired faces were soaked in pure feeling, each dripping with their own memories of love and heartache. For a brief time they were not robots of the morning, but had come alive.

The music filled them with its sadness and longing. And when it stopped there was a second of silence before every single person clapped.

Uncle bowed.

'More, more!' came a chorus of voices.

Uncle beamed and shook his head. 'I got a café to run. Maybe tomorrow.'

He disappeared into the kitchen, which now seemed to have the glamour of backstage. The café, which had been almost quiet before, was abuzz with conversation. Uncle had lifted them all.

'Not bad for a cook, eh?,' said Ringer.

'Brilliant,' exclaimed Roy. 'Does he do it a lot?'

'When he's in the mood. Sometimes he won't sing for a week – then does it every day. Depends how he's getting on with Maisie. Me aunt.'

31

Roy was still amazed. 'I just can't believe it. I've never been so close to that sort of singing before. I mean he just came out and did it.' To Roy, who was shy, and thought over everything twice, it was the bravest thing he had ever seen.

'Yeh,' said Ringer. 'That's Uncle.' He stood up. 'Things to do.'

Roy was disappointed; he wanted to talk some more. He tried not to show it.

'You off, then?'

'I gotta go. Mum wants me to look after the twins. Pesky nuisance the pair of them. It's what I hate about school holidays. See you tomorrow, eh?'

'Thanks for the help.'

Ringer gave him a thumbs-up as he left the café.

In a very few seconds Roy felt uncomfortable. He was on his own with grown-ups all around. He felt as if every eye was on him, when plainly they weren't. Uncle was busy buttering toast. Ordinary again, as if he was nothing to do with the man who had held them all spellbound only two minutes before. The various men dotted around had gone back to eating and reading papers. Roy just had the feeling that he shouldn't be here. Not without Ringer.

Or maybe he'd said too much.

Roy quickly finished the fried bread, knocked back his cooling tea, and left.

Chapter 8

He saw the wheel sticking out from under a parked car – just a bit of the tyre and the ends of a few spokes. He pulled it out and found it was intact. It had the thick tyre of a mountain bike and was pumped up hard. A front wheel – there were no gear wheels on the hub – and it had a quick-release lever. Roy wondered where the rest of the bike was, probably chained to a railing. Quick release was fine in a race if you wanted to change wheels in a hurry – but it also meant anyone could undo it with their fingers, and plainly someone had.

He held it up and rolled it round in his fingers. A new bike; the tyre was hardly worn and the spokes and hub were shiny. Probably cost a few bob too. He put it down on the pavement and patted it along with him as he walked, like a hoop. Just the odd touch was enough to keep it running alongside.

Roy was up with the leaders but had been holding back for this section of the race, the mountains. Everyone had marvelled that his bike was just an ordinary bike, a shop-bought one, instead of the superbikes especially made for the top riders in this, the Tour de France. It's not the bike he had told them – it's the rider. And now in the mountains it was time to show them.

He was with the pack as they started to climb. Roy began to push, standing high on the pedals. Around him the pack began to break as riders fell back unable to stay the pace. And still he pushed, climbing up the mountain road. He could hear the few still with him, their fierce pained breath, a glance to the side showed in their strained faces just how much it was hurting. Now he thought – and gave it the little bit he had left. And like a train pulling out of the station he began to leave them behind, the sound of their wheels and voices gradually getting lost as the distance increased. Yes, it was hurting. The mountains always hurt, they seemed to go up for ever – but steadily he kept

up the pressure, going away up the incline. Up and up to the summit
that was hidden in the clouds . . .

He was alone in his kingdom, the mountains. Here he was unbeat-
able, King of the Mountains. There were weeks more of the Tour de
France yet but if he built up a big enough lead in the mountains then
the Tour would be his. An Englishman had never won before. Roy felt
back to his saddlebag. He squeezed it. Yes, it was there, the bone-
spanner. . .

He took the wheel into the house. He thought of leaving it in
the main hallway but then changed his mind. It would be so
easy for the lady downstairs to chuck it out. So he took it into
the flat, and left it inside by the front door.

The flat was silent. His mother wasn't up. Roy wasn't hungry
– the fried bread had filled him – and so he went to his room.
He wondered whether he should go back to bed, but didn't
want to do that now he was up. Yet he felt lonely by himself –
and could carry on his dream in bed. King of the Mountains.

Didn't he have a picture of that? Where was it? He went
through a box of bike magazines and posters, unfolding them
all on the floor. He had bought them all at a car boot sale for £2.
Mum thought he'd been robbed, but there were years of magazines. All technical stuff, and articles about races. And full of
photos, plus all the posters.

There it was. A picture of the pack climbing some rocky
mountains – and just ahead a single rider. It was a front-on
shot, slightly at an angle, so you could see their straining faces
and also their bikes.

Roy stuck it on the wall. Then he went through the other
posters. He had a large one of a racing bike with all the different bits labelled. That had to go up. And another of the
Olympic pursuit, the two riders on the small track chasing
each other. And of course the one of the mountain bike leaping
the stream . . . That had to go up.

All through the morning he covered the walls, and then
with his energy still high he put his clothes away in the drawers and in his small wardrobe. A little later on he glanced out

the window – there was the old man in the next-door garden hoeing between rows of cabbages. He felt akin to him; each of them in their own space. For the room was surely his now. And perhaps if he had a hook he could hang the bike wheel on the wall?

Or the ceiling. Then he could tie things to the wheel and spin it.

Thinking of the wheel made him think of the bike he would get. And he would. He was determined. He had done the paper round this morning, and at £14 per week in three weeks . . .? £42. That would get him a bike of sorts. Something that would go at least and that he could do up – because he'd still be earning each week. Week by week he could replace the tyres, the brake blocks, the cables, get new mudguards, lights, a lock, toe clips, build up a stock of tools, a pannier . . . He could rub down the paintwork and give it a repaint. He could start with an ordinary bike – all right, a less than ordinary bike; it had to be admitted £42 wasn't that much, but as long as the frame was OK and the wheels were in good nick – and over time he could build on it. And he'd found a wheel . . . so if the front wheel wasn't up to much he could replace it.

That was the thing about bikes. You could find or swap or buy the bits and do it yourself. All you needed was a book – he knew there were bike books in the library. But that was another thing he could buy – his own bicycle manual. Instead of getting it out the library, he'd have it with him whenever he wanted it. He wouldn't have to return it and pay fines, and find when he really needed it someone else had it out. But with his own – say two o'clock in the morning if he wanted to check out something on gears – then lights on, and go to it.

It was starting to happen. After the move was now! He'd worked one day already. That meant he'd earned £2. Just £40 to go. His excitement growing, Roy took an old poster he wasn't that keen on. He turned it over and with a ruler he drew a long oblong tower. At the bottom of the tower, just inside, he wrote £2. Then he put a line above and then wrote

£4, and a line above that. Then £6 and a line, then £8, and so on until he got to £42. He drew a last line and on this line he sketched a bicycle with a little flag on it.

He stuck the paper on the wall and stepped back. It was like a lighthouse starting at £2, the £2 he earned today, and going up the tower to the magic number – and at the top, of course, the bike. There were twenty-one boxes with numbers in – and he'd already done the first. He got a red pencil and coloured the bottom box. Twenty days to go. *Only* twenty days to go.

He was impatient for it to be tomorrow morning – so he could colour the second. Then nineteen to go. He imagined the red swallowing up the days as it rose up the tower. Until – bike day on day 21.

It was going to happen. He could feel it. Then he had an idea. He drew an arrow pointing to between day 10 and day 11 on his tower. At the end of the arrow he wrote 'Half a bike'.

He'd be at *Half a bike* in no time.

Tomorrow he just had to get up in the morning and do the round. And he had Ringer to help out. It had been a good morning. He hadn't got lost on the paper round or had to lie to Mr Patel, he'd met Ringer and had fried bread with him. Found a wheel. And don't forget the bone spanner . . . His lucky bone spanner.

Twenty days to go. He held the little spanner and closed his eyes. Twenty days.

Ten days to *Half a bike*. Well, nine and a half – but say ten.

Around one o'clock he began feeling hungry and went to the kitchen. His mother was still not up. He wondered what to have. Maybe he should ask.

He went to her room and knocked lightly.

'Come in,' came a voice that was half a groan.

Opening the door carefully he put his head round. A fug of drink and tobacco hit him. His mother lay in bed in a muss of bedclothes, her hair straggly and her face washed out. She looked old and worn-out, her skin saggy and pale. By the side of the bed was an empty bottle of whisky.

'You wouldn't make me a cup of tea, would you, love? And I think I left some fags by the fridge. There – be a dear, Roy.'

He went to make the tea, his heart suddenly down in his boots.

Chapter 9

Uncle was busy when they entered. There were the usual people. Roy was beginning to recognise them after his fourth morning on the round. One or two even smiled as they came in. A man in the corner gave a half wave.

'Morning, lads.'

Ringer ordered. Roy sat down at a window table and began to calculate. Four days meant eight quid. That was nearly a fifth of a bike. It still seemed a long time to get to the top of his tower. Another seventeen days. But then he'd have £42. Surely he would find some kid moving up to a better bike and wanting to get rid of the old one, or someone who just wasn't using theirs any more. But seventeen more days of getting up in the morning, seventeen more days of setting off with the bag . . . He stretched his back and rubbed his neck.

Ringer came back with two teas. 'Mr Patel's moaning about you.'

'Yeh.'

'What's the problem?'

Roy shrugged. 'Just no good at getting up. The alarm goes off, then I look at the clock, I think ten more minutes . . . Next time I open my eyes again – help! And I have to steam out of the house still dressing.'

'He said twenty minutes today, fifteen yesterday . . .'

'But I rushed through that round today. I bet I made up the time.'

Ringer shook his head. 'He'll sack you.'

Roy bit his lip.

'He will. You have to get straight up when the alarm goes off. None of this ten more minutes stuff.'

'Yeh, all right.' Roy knew Ringer was right but hated being

lectured. 'Where's that fried bread? I'm starving.' He cuddled his hands round the cup of tea and took a sip. And shuddered with the first heat.

'I asked Uncle to do the Toreador song,' Ringer whispered. 'He said he might. Cross fingers.'

'How does he learn all the words?'

'He's got books. CDs. Goes to classes.'

'What's your mum think of his singing?'

'She loves it. Goes with him to the opera sometimes. His wife won't go. She says it's just for fat Italians.'

'It's not,' protested Roy.

"Course not. It's just to have a go at him. If he likes something – then she doesn't.'

'Why did he marry her?'

'Why did my mum marry my dad? Why did your mum marry yours?'

'They fell in love.'

'And then fell in love with someone else.' Seeing Roy's face he added quickly. 'Sorry, Roy. But he did – didn't he?'

'Something like that.'

He went for his tea again. He could hardly remember what his dad looked like. He might pass him in the street and not know. But then – would his dad recognise him? Roy had changed so much in six years. He'd been just a kid then. No, he had to admit it; they'd be strangers to each other.

A wave of emptiness went through him.

Uncle was doing a round with a tray, dropping off the plates of this and that with his usual familiarity.

'One fried bread, one toast and jam, Roy, Ringer. One rendition of the Toreador song.'

Uncle stepped back and put the tray on the counter. Over one shoulder was a tea cloth. He clapped his hands and addressed the café.

'Ladies and gentlemen!'

Heads looked up from newspapers, knives and forks froze mid-air, conversation ceased.

'My friends! I was born in East London but I wish I was born in Italy. Because Italy is the land of opera – and one day I shall close this café and go to Milan. Then every day I will go to La Scala, the opera house. In the meantime I shall sing opera here for you.'

There were catcalls, whistles and cheers.

Uncle held up his hands for silence. He waited for it and, when there was not a sound to be heard, he began the Toreador song. He sang it grandly, with broad gestures, loudly as if the café were a many-tiered theatre. When he got to the march in the middle, he drew down his tea towel and had a mock bullfight across the café. Roy was surprised at his agility, that he could move and sing simultaneously. Uncle was large, fat you might say – but it didn't matter that he wore his café apron, that his cape was a tea cloth; he had the proud grace of the toreador.

The music swirled and transported. Workmen with the day ahead smiled, hurt and loss discarded, sons abandoned by fathers forgot. There was only the music: music that soothed, that bathed, that, like a nurse, made everything better.

The applause came like water rushing through a dam. Uncle lapped it up. The claps, the cheers; he waved to everyone, smiling broadly as if they were an audience of two thousand at La Scala. Then with a final bow he put his hands up for quiet, thanked them all – and went to buttering bread behind the counter.

'Your uncle is amazing.'

Ringer gave a toothy grin.

'It's such big music,' added Roy.

'Well he's not exactly a little fella,' said Ringer with a laugh.

Roy looked behind to make sure Uncle wasn't there, then whispered, 'He reminds me of Popeye.'

'Popeye can't sing like that,' said Ringer in mock affront.

'Yeh, but give Uncle a sailor's hat and a little pipe . . .'

'Talking of pipes . . .' interrupted Ringer. 'What you doing tomorrow afternoon?'

'Not a lot. Why?'

'It's low tide at four.'

Roy couldn't make much of this information. 'So?'

'Wanna come up the riverside?'

'Well. All right.'

'I wanna get some pipes.'

'Pipes?' Roy still couldn't get to grips with this. 'What sort of pipes?'

Ringer grinned. 'Don't you like surprises? Come along. You might like it.' He shrugged. 'And if you don't – put it down to experience. Got any wellies?'

'No.'

'I'll bring you a pair.' Ringer stood up. 'Things to do.'

'You off then?' Ringer always left Roy wanting more.

'I'll call for you at three.'

And Roy was left with his slice of fried bread.

Chapter 10

He was on top of the mountain where it was cold and wild and rocky. This was the roof of the world. Behind him, not even in sight, were the 200 riders of the pack, the world's best, whom he had broken on the uphill climb. But even up here, alone, he would not give back an inch that he had won on the climb.

The road began to descend. The slope began leisurely, and then he rounded a bend, and without warning, the downhill began in earnest. There was no need to pedal, he just had to hold the bike to the road, as it went down and round the mountain curves. He did not touch the brakes but went with the flow, at whatever speed it took him. On one side was cliff, on the other a sheer drop of two thousand metres. In the distance, on the wind, he could just hear a brass band playing. There would be bunting and cheering. Union Jacks would be waving as he flew off the mountain into the streets of the town . . .

A motorbike overtook him on a tight bend, then slowed a little way in front. The man on the back had a TV camera and was shooting him in close-up, amazed that such an old bike, costing just £42, could be ridden by the leader in the Tour de France . . .

Roy opened his eyes and blinked in the harsh light. He was about to duck under the blankets again when he looked at the clock. Oh no! Couldn't be! He had just closed his eyes for a few minutes when he shut off the alarm. Surely not? How could time go so fast!

He threw off the blankets and was out of bed. It seemed just minutes ago when the alarm went off. Now he was going to be . . . He quickly calculated: five minutes to get dressed and out the house, then he'd have to sprint like crazy down the road. About fifteen minutes late again. What was he going to say to Mr Patel this time?

And what would Mr Patel say to him!

His pyjamas were a puddle on the floor as he pulled on his underwear. Shirt? Where was his shirt? Mum must have taken it. Did he have a clean one? He went through the chest of drawers. Pants, vests, hankies – no shirts. They must be all in the wash. Why didn't she ever wash anything?

He found a T-shirt. It needed ironing, well too bad for that. He had tie-dyed it in pink at that youth club, must be two years ago. Horrible, ice-cream pink but that was the only colour they had. He drew it over his head and down. It was tight under the armpits and across the chest. Too tight; he'd grown in two years. He couldn't wear this yucky thing; he could hardly move in it.

He raced out of his room, into the hallway and into the bathroom. What was that horrible smell? The dirty-linen basket was full to the brim, with bits and pieces scattered around it, too much to all go in. He pulled out yesterday's shirt. That would do. Bit grubby round the collar – but so what? He was only doing a paper round.

Back in the bedroom, Roy pulled off the pink T-shirt, put yesterday's shirt on and his trousers. Socks? He searched under the bed. She must've taken his socks as well. He shook his fists in rage. Then went through the chest of drawers and came up with one brown sock. Another search, scrabbling through clothes, and he came up with a blue one.

He had to wear socks as his trainers gave him blisters without. No one would notice if he had one brown and one blue. And if they did he'd say it was a new fashion. Or he'd say, that's funny, I've got another pair exactly like this at home.

Make a joke of it.

Trainers on.

A shoelace broke. Heck. His clumsy, still tired fingers, knotted it. He knew there wouldn't be any spares.

Roy glanced at the clock and wished he hadn't. All that messing around with shirts and shoelaces; he was going to be at least twenty minutes late.

He must have some juice before he left. He'd take it straight from the carton; Mum hated him doing that, but she wouldn't be up to see. He sprinted out of his room and into the hall. Time was racing by. The sitting room door was shut. He flung himself through it, feeling resistance but going too fast to stop. The door opened, there was a scream as he ran into a stepladder.

All the world dropped on him.

At the end of a headlong second Roy was on the floor, the ladder splayed out and his mother lying on her back. Roy sat up, his eyes watering. His elbow was bruised, and head throbbing where he'd hit the ladder. He rubbed his arm wondering whether he had broken something, saw his mother and crawled over to her.

'You all right?' he said, seeing at once that she wasn't.

She was trying to sit up, pushing her chest, gasping as if something was stuck there.

Roy watched helplessly as she slapped one arm behind her back. She did it again, looking at him in appeal – and he got the idea.

Roy went behind and gave her a slap. She nodded furiously. He did it again.

'More,' she said huskily.

He slapped her a couple more times.

His mother signalled him to stop, then struggled to her feet, pressing her ribs and twisting.

'Where the heck did you come from?' she managed to say.

'I just came in to get a drink . . .'

'And knocked me flying . . .' She suddenly screamed: 'The paint!'

A large can of paint was lying sideways on the carpet. Most of the paint had poured out and was flowing along the carpet, thick, sticky and very white.

Mum, uselessly, righted the can.

He looked at her plaintively. 'I gotta go, Mum.'

She ignored him. 'Get me that old torn sheet in the airing cupboard . . .'

'I gotta go!'

'You knocked me flat!' she yelled.

'I couldn't help it if you were painting . . .'

'Do you have to go sprinting around the house? Get me the old torn sheet . . .'

Roy rushed off to the airing cupboard, just outside the bathroom. He rested his aching head on the door and rubbed his throbbing elbow. He pulled his arm backwards and forwards; it hurt but moved; he'd be able to lift his bag. For a second he forgot what he had come out for.

The sheet.

He opened the cupboard; the torn sheet was lying in a heap at the bottom. He ran back with it to the sitting room, where his mother was trying to mop up the paint with a magazine.

'Get the old newspapers.'

'I gotta go, Mum.'

'Don't argue with everything I say. Get them.'

He went back into the hall where there was a pile of newspaper. They'd brought them from the other house. He'd thought it was stupid bringing them but Mum said they'd be useful. He grabbed an armful. It seemed she was right.

Back in the sitting room he dropped the pile.

'Fill both buckets for me,' she said.

'Mum!'

'Get me water!' she yelled. 'Anyone would think I knocked you down. Now get me water! And lots of it.'

Roy went to the bathroom. He just had to get out of the house. No matter what she said. Mr Patel would be going crazy.

He trudged back into the sitting room weighed down with a bucket at the end of each arm.

'Mop up as much as you can,' she said, seated in an island of newspaper and laying out more. 'Before it settles in.'

'I gotta go,' he beseeched her. 'Please, Mum – I really have to.'

'Go then!' she yelled at him. 'You're no help at all. You've spilt the paint, busted the ladder. Look at it!'

45

'It never was much good.'

'You've broken the upright.'

'It was cracked.'

'And now it's useless.'

'Please, Mum – I gotta go. I'll lose my job . . .'

'Just go then!'

He knew she didn't really want him to – but he went.

It was only when he was out in the hallway that he saw he was covered in paint. He'd been kneeling in it. Paint was on his shoes. Paint was on his hands and fingernails. Blobs of it, streaks of it.

Back in the bathroom Roy tried to sponge his trousers off. And then when he'd already got them soaking wet, he gave up on them; he had simply spread the colour, they had become milky white. He took them off and searched through the dirty washing for another pair. Then for a shirt and socks.

His shoes were sticky with paint. He wiped them as best he could with toilet roll. Over the tops, the sides and underneath where he'd walked in it. Enough he thought, it'll have to do. And unlocked the bathroom door.

'Roy,' she called as she saw him in the hall, 'be a dear, get me . . .'

'No,' he yelled, not waiting to hear what she wanted, as he crashed down the stairs. 'I'm already too late!'

Shutting the flat door, he flew through the short hallway, opened the street door and slammed it hard against the jamb as his last word to her.

Chapter 11

'Please, Mr Patel.'

He was still breathless, standing at the counter of the newsagent's, his chest heaving. 'It wasn't my fault. My mum . . .' Roy hesitated then added, 'She was ill. I would've been early. But she was really ill.'

'And was she ill yesterday?'

'No.'

'And the day before?'

'No, but . . .'

The Indian man held up his hands to stop him, palms pale brown. 'I'm not interested in excuses . . .'

They were interrupted by a woman buying a magazine and some sweets. Roy had a stitch from his flat-out sprint to the shop. He rubbed his ribs down to his waist as he waited for the newsagent to finish.

'Here you are.'

Mr Patel was holding out some notes.

'What's that?'

'Payment for the days you worked.' He pressed the money. 'Take it, please. Eight pounds for four days.'

Roy took it and thrust it in his back pocket.

'Please give me another chance.'

The newsagent shook his head. 'I warned you when you came. Remember?'

'Yes, but . . .'

'I told you what I wanted. What I have to have. I'm running a business here. I have to keep my customers happy. When a boy's late – they get their newspapers late. And they want them before they go to work. If they don't get them they cancel.'

'Let me do the round – I'll go like the wind.'

'Do the round!' the newsagent exploded. 'Do you think I've still got the papers here, when you are more than an hour late?'

Roy was struck dumb.

'I gave them to one of the boys who had finished.' He hammered on the counter with his fist. 'Finished! And you not even here! Now go away.'

'Please, Mr Patel – I give you my word . . .'

Another customer came between them. Roy waited impatiently for him to buy his cigarettes and newspaper. He mustn't be sacked. He had to convince Mr Patel it wouldn't happen again.

'You're blocking the shop,' said the newsagent when the customer had gone. 'Please go.'

'Just give me one chance.'

'No.' The newsagent began tidying some football cards on the counter.

'It won't ever happen again. I promise.'

'And I think it will.' He looked up, his face hard set, dark brown eyes reflecting the outside window.

'I admit those other days were my fault . . .' Roy tried desperately. 'But today, honest . . .' Tears welled in his eyes. 'My mum was ill.'

The newsagent had gone back to straightening cards. Quietly he said, 'I am not a charity. I am running a business. I told you what I expected of you – and you weren't able to give it.' He held up his hands, 'I have nothing against you personally – but you are repeatedly late. And that makes problems for me. And I have enough problems already.'

'But I need the job.'

'I'm sorry about that, but I don't need you.'

'Please.'

'No.' He turned his back to tidy the cigarettes in the shelves behind him. 'And that's my last word.'

'I'll never be late again.'

No reply from the bustling back.

48

'I'll do a day for nothing.' In desperation he added, 'Two days. Three . . .'

The newsagent worked on. It was as if he had not spoken.

'Please, please, please . . . Mr Patel. Please.'

Another customer came and another. The newsagent would not look at Roy standing by the rack of stationery. Clearly it was at an end; Mr Patel would not be moved.

There was nothing Roy could say. With tear-filled eyes he left the shop.

Chapter 12

He ran away from the high street, the scene of his shame. A cauldron of anger and hurt bubbled within him, tears changing to rage. How he hated her! He wished she was dead. *She* had done it. Her and her all-night painting had got him sacked.

She had lost him his bike.

He wished he was an orphan with no mother to humiliate him. He thought of himself as dead, no – as dying, of some terrible disease that had in some way been brought on by her. Her behaviour brought on a brainstorm (he'd read the words in a story once) and the brainstorm grew worse because she went on and on, ignoring the fact that he was growing weaker and was developing a fever. Until he collapsed. And even then she wouldn't do the washing and stayed up all night painting the sitting room, then the bedrooms, then the hall . . . And she smoked all the housekeeping money instead of buying proper food. While he grew weaker and weaker from neglect.

Until even she, even she, had to call a doctor. Or perhaps it was someone else who called the doctor. And the doctor said, 'Your son is dying.'

Then how sorry she was. As he lay on his deathbed with life seeping out of him, she wept and said how wrong she had been. And he answered not a word. She begged him to speak but he simply looked up at the ceiling, letting her go on and on. It was too late for excuses.

Then she brought his father. He too begged Roy's forgiveness, and Roy just looked at him out of his sunken eyes, and said nothing. Mr Patel came to the house. He said he was sorry he had sacked him; he hadn't realised at the time how important the job was to him. The job was his any time he wanted it.

And Roy said nothing to his mother and father, and Mr Patel – all entreating him round his sick bed. Now let them suffer for their neglect. And then he died, and tears filled the house. His mother wandered about saying, 'If only . . .' into her tear-filled handkerchief.

At his funeral it rained . . .

Here he stopped. There would be too few at his funeral. The world would not be sorry. The world wouldn't even know. He kicked a wall. He punched a tree.

In this fantasy of hate Roy had followed no particular direction. As he went down streets and crossed roads the anger in him flared, seeking more fuel, like a forest fire grabbing every tree and sapling in its path.

Who else had a mother who spent all night painting? All night! And was still doing it at seven in the morning . . . How did she expect him to know she was up there on a ladder? Then shouting at him and making him get sheets, water, newspaper . . . until he was covered in paint himself.

And lost his job.

Did she never think of him?

Roy came to a park with large wrought-iron gates. He peered through them and saw paths and seats and bins, and leafy trees running along the paths that ran off – he didn't know where. To places. The world was full of places, and whenever you got there you found more paths going off. Maybe then there wasn't any point going anywhere. Maybe you might as well stay in bed. Or get drunk.

But then every place wasn't the same. And didn't they give you a chance to do something? A new chance.

Didn't they?

But how could you get to these new places?

Roy entered and slumped in a seat. Was he always going to be stuck here? Within shouting distance of his mother.

A voice said, 'You still want that bike?'

He looked up. It was the boy with the mountain bike, the £300 bike, that he had met a couple of days ago.

'My mate says he'll bring his bike round.'

Roy made no reply but looked at the boy's bike. The sleek black frame, the three chain-wheels, the toe clips. He wanted to push him off and take it. That boy who got everything for the asking. He, Roy, should have that bike.

'So you interested?'

'No.'

'I thought you said . . .'

'I don't want your mate's rubbish.'

'Well, I admit it's not like this one. But what d'you expect for seventy . . .'

'Junk. Forget it. I want a bike. A real one.' He was up and striding off.

A voice from behind called, 'So I'll tell him you're not interested?'

'You tell him!' he shouted back, then didn't turn again.

He knew now where he was going. He knew what he was going to do. It was the only way he could be free and take control in the world. The only way he could take the paths away, up, out. Take the chances instead of everyone jumping on him in these crabby streets.

He was going to get a bike.

Chapter 13

'Can I use your loo?'

Uncle looked up from his counter where he was reading a paper.

'Sure, Roy.'

Roy thanked him and strode through into the kitchen. Then through the kitchen to the back room. Making sure Uncle wasn't watching, he quietly opened the cupboard. Quickly he took out the bolt-cutters, shut the cupboard and went into the loo.

He locked the toilet door, and leaned hard against the wall breathing heavily with relief. He had with him a carrier bag containing newspaper and string that he had picked up from a litter bin along the way; he put it on the floor and examined the bolt-cutters.

They were beautiful. He worked the jaws with the handles. He could imagine them cutting anything. A chain, a lock.

On the way to Uncle's he had planned what to do. The carrier, papers and string were to get the bolt-cutters out of the café. They weren't small, you couldn't just slip them in your pocket, or even up your sleeve without looking like you'd broken your arm. So he needed something to get them past Uncle. Then after that he'd thought out likely places. And he'd passed one on the way here. It was as if everything was working for him.

He'd come by the swimming baths, and outside were bikes chained up to a row of cycle stands. There'd been five bikes there. Some with D-locks – well he'd never get through one of those – but a couple of them had cheap chains. One of them appalled him. A bike like that must have cost nearly two hundred – and then using a couple-of-quid lock. The kid deserved to have it nicked.

Sinking to the floor, Roy took the newspaper out of the carrier bag and wrapped it loosely round the bolt-cutters. Then more paper, lots of sheets, so the shape got lost, then he tied string round so the cutters wouldn't unwrap. Finally he put the untidy parcel in the carrier bag.

Dirty work done, he got up and pulled the toilet handle. He let the water run and then left the toilet. He was about to go through the kitchen when he remembered. This had to look genuine; so he stopped and washed his hands.

While wiping them, he steeled himself for the encounter with Uncle. Keep it brief. It had to be straight through the kitchen, a wave to Uncle, then out.

The kitchen was easy. Uncle was still reading at the counter as he entered the café.

'Thanks,' said Roy.

'Wanna cup of tea?'

He should have just said no. He should have said that he had to get back to his mum, but instead he hesitated.

'You can't be in that much of a hurry.'

He was, but he couldn't admit it.

'All right,' said Roy. 'Just a quick one.'

Uncle poured two cups of tea. 'Want a cheese roll?'

'Well I dunno . . .'

'I'm having one. You have one.'

'All right,' said Roy. He couldn't summon up the energy to refuse.

Uncle brought the tea and rolls out to a table and beckoned Roy to take a seat. Roy did so, keeping the carrier bag under the table and out of sight.

'Been shopping?'

'Yeh.' He felt the need to say more. 'For Mum. Some stuff from the charity shop. I don't know what it is.'

'Let's have a look,' Uncle said.

'It's all wrapped up.'

'Never mind then.' Uncle took a sip of tea and a bite of roll. 'First break I've had all day.' Out of a yawn he added, 'How d'you like it round here?'

'Don't really know yet.'

'How's your mum taking it?'

'All right.'

'Got any brothers or sisters?'

'Just me.' He put his foot against the bag. He wanted to get out of the shop badly but had to go through with this now. He tried eating the roll. He didn't want it, he was too nervous for food. But he had to eat it now.

'Me and Maisie wanted kids.' Uncle took a swig of tea. 'Didn't work out. She couldn't get pregnant. One doctor says it was me. Another says it's her. But her or me, or both . . .' He opened his hands helplessly. 'That's the way it goes.'

Roy had another go at the roll. He felt sick.

'She worked here once.' He shook his head. 'Mistake. We couldn't get away from each other. Here, then home. Disaster.'

Uncle was looking across the café, shaking his head, as if imagining his wife there. Roy held his stomach in to keep the roll down.

'She had different ideas for this place. Wanted to go upmarket. Open up in the evenings, subdued lighting, tablecloths. Lasagne, moussaka – all sorts of stuff. Well, I can't cook that. I do fried bread, fry-ups, this and that with chips or mash. My idea was to cater for workmen. Breakfast in the morning, then lunch – whatever you do, give 'em lots of potatoes; it doesn't pay to skimp on the chips. I mean, potatoes are cheap enough. And then tea – and close around five-thirty. But she wanted us to close in the afternoon and open in the evening for the posh trade. She talked me into it, she wore me down. In the end we were working eighteen hours a day. In a restaurant you've got to make so many dishes. We had to have another cook, and a waitress. It was non-stop. I never seemed to be out of the place. And me and Maisie were arguing all the time. About the food, about why we weren't making money, about the staff . . . Then Maisie got ill. And I couldn't run it on my own. So I went back to this. To what I knew. You all right?'

'Just – not very hungry.'

'Leave it then.' Uncle swallowed the last piece of his own roll, and followed up with a sip of tea. 'It turned out the cook and waitress were robbing us. Doing a fiddle on the till. Maisie wanted me to call the police. I thought what's the point – we'll never get the money back . . .' Uncle stopped, his eyes narrowing. 'Horrible time. And we never got over it. Not really. All that fighting. Bookkeeping at one in the morning when you have to be up at six. Both blaming each other. You say a lot of things, and then you can't unsay 'em. You see a side of a person you find you don't like at all.' Uncle threw back the tea and looked at his watch. 'Whatever you do – never live and work with someone. Take my advice.'

'I liked your singing,' attempted Roy.

'That's another thing with me and Maisie . . .' He halted with a wry laugh. 'You don't want to listen to me going on?'

'I do. It's interesting.' And at some other time it might really have been – but the carrier bag was pressing into his leg. He wondered if he could stand up without trembling. How would he ever get out of here?

The café door opened and a customer came in.

Uncle sighed. 'No peace for the wicked.'

He got up and went to the counter and began to talk to the customer.

Roy rose. His legs were jelly.

'Bye,' he managed to say. 'Thanks.'

And was out of the door and onto the street. He thought of running but then doubted if he could. He must just walk steadily.

He hadn't gone very far when there was a call from behind.

'Roy!'

He turned. Uncle was standing at the door of the shop holding up the carrier bag.

'You forgot this!'

Chapter 14

The only way Roy knew to the Baths was past the house. There were other ways, there had to be. Probably quicker ways, but he'd only gone there from the house.

He thought about the words. *The* house.

How long would it be before he called it *my* house? Mum and he used to say our flats, meaning the estate, and our flat, meaning the one they lived in. This was *the* house. He felt it was going to be 'the' for a long time.

But if you lived there long enough – then would you start saying 'my', because anything else had faded away, and there had to be somewhere that was yours? Even if you didn't like it much.

He would walk swiftly past when he got there. He'd had enough of his mum for some time. Didn't want to see her. So straight to the Baths, no messing. Get the bike, then take the bolt-cutters back. How would he get them past Uncle? He'd made him sweat enough first time round. Sitting at the table being told about Uncle's life at the café, trying to eat that roll, with the bag pressing against his leg so hard that it was almost surprising that Uncle couldn't feel it too. And then having to go back for the bag. Uncle holding it up for him and making a joke about next time forgetting his head. Walking back to get it he couldn't look Uncle in the eye.

Did he notice?

Must've done. When Roy took the bag off him he must've seen. Must've guessed from his shiftiness that he was up to something. Or did he just think the boy was shy? Or that . . . the boy was going out to steal a bicycle?

No – not that. Uncle wasn't a mind reader. Probably making a sandwich now and whistling a tune from opera. Roy crossed his fingers that Uncle wouldn't notice that the cutters were missing.

He was near his house now. Up ahead was the boy with the bike. What was his name? Three hundred pounds he would call him. The boy was sitting on the wall, the bike leaning against it. The boy watched Roy approach.

'He sold it,' said the boy. 'For fifty.'

'I thought he wanted seventy.'

The boy shrugged. 'He just wanted to get rid of it. But I reckon he could've got seventy or eighty.'

'Someone got a bargain.'

'Yeh.' The boy hesitated a second then said, 'Do you know anything about gears?'

'A bit.'

'Well these are slipping.'

Roy got down and looked at the gear cogs. He could see the article in the magazine on chain and gears. Points to remember.

He felt the chain.

'This is too tight.'

'You think so?'

'Probably not the trouble, though. Just might snap on you one day.'

'Then what?'

'Then you'll have to push it home. This is it. This cable. It's too loose. You're probably not getting half your gears.'

'That's right.'

'Twenty-one gears you should have.'

'Twenty-one? You sure?'

'Seven cogs in the back block, three chain wheels. Three sevens are twenty-one. That's twenty-one gears.' He could see the boy looked puzzled. He didn't deserve a bike. Fancy having one and knowing nothing about it. 'Each one of these chain-wheels can work with any of the back seven. So it's seven plus seven plus seven.'

'I get it.'

'Now if I turn this.' He had his fingers on the cable-adjusting barrel coming out of the rear derailleur. 'It's got a lot of slack in it. Try that. You'll have to go for a ride. I reckon it'll work but you might have to turn it back and forth a bit to get it dead on. This here.'

'What's it called?'

'It's just the cable adjuster.'

'How do you know all this?'

'Magazines . . .' He ran his fingers up a gear cable to where it came out of the lever on the handlebars. 'Bikes I've had,' he lied. 'Taken to bits, put back together . . . They're just machines. It's all got to connect.'

'Some of the time I was pedalling and nothing was turning.'

'Go for a ride now.'

The boy got on and cycled down the pavement. Roy watched him and then turned away. He hated that boy. He always seemed to be here waiting, with the bike he knew nothing about. There was always someone who got the best of everything. And always someone else who got nothing. Why was the world set up like that? Why was he born with a mum who smoked and drank? Why couldn't he have parents who would spend £300 on him? *He'd* read books on bikes, not that boy. He would appreciate it. Not that boy. Why did the wrong people get things?

Suddenly the boy whizzed past. 'Hey – they're working! Thanks!'

The boy bumped off the pavement onto the road. Roy tried hard not to look at him. In fact he'd had enough of him. Him and his bike. Roy strode quickly up the road. He was near his house now. Straight on he'd go and on to the Baths.

It was his turn.

Roy began to run, the carrier bag bashing against his leg. Faster before the boy got back and gave a greater display of his ignorance. The more stupid you are the better bike you get, it seemed.

Well, he'd change that.

He slowed up just before his house, winded. Walking past he saw Ringer at the door.

'Hey!' called Ringer. 'I been buzzing for five minutes.'

Roy stopped. Ringer was wearing a pair of wellington boots, carrying another pair, and had on a backpack. Roy vaguely remembered something he'd agreed to. Yesterday at the café. What the heck was it?

'You set then?' Seeing Roy's puzzlement he added, 'Going up the river. You said you'd come.'

Ringer waited, his face screwed up, trying to read Roy's silence.

'You don't have to.'

Roy caught the edge of disappointment. He thought of the Baths and the row of bikes. He saw himself kneeling with the cutters.

'I'll go on me own if you don't want to,' said Ringer.

Something evaporated, something burned off. Or perhaps it was just the fact of being asked. Of being wanted. There are just times not to say no.

Roy got out his keys. 'Just let me drop this carrier bag off. Eh?'

Chapter 15

'Here. Down these steps.'

There was a break in the railings and a set of concrete steps going down to a stony beach. The top of the steps was clean but the lower end was covered in green waterweed, drying out in the sun.

The boys went down, on to a stony beach.

'It's all right here on the stones,' said Ringer. 'It's those muddy patches you have to watch. Some of them are dead deep.'

'I've never been down here,' said Roy gazing at the wide hemisphere of river and beach.

'Hardly anyone has. Grandad used to bring me. He was a sailor and used to say this was as near as he could get to the sea. He started bringing me when Dad's trial was on. It was in the newspapers every day and Mum was going to the court. There was a lot of fuss, and so Grandad used to bring me down here. To get away from everyone.'

The waves slipped back and forth at the river's edge. A group of ducks were paddling nearby and gulls wheeling above. Most of the river was empty though, with just a few tied-up barges, and then nothing across the several hundred metres of brown water. Except to the right, where two fat ferries loaded with lorries and cars were about to pass in mid river.

"S'all right here,' said Roy.

'You hardly see anyone. Sometimes a guy with a metal detector but mostly no one.'

They walked slowly along the shore, still on the stony area. It was like a real beach with the stones rounded and smooth and patches of sand here and there.

'It's low tide,' said Ringer. 'In a few hours it'll all be covered. See that weed?' He pointed to the sloping defences built at the edge of the beach that were covered to two thirds of their height in green. 'The water gets up to that green. Every day this beach is covered and uncovered twice.'

Roy picked up a bit of glass. It had gone all frosty and the edges rounded. It had a rough sandy feel.

'Used to be really busy up here,' Ringer went on. 'Thirty, forty years ago. There'd be ships and everything going up the river. Well, when the tide was high, that is. Going to all the London Docks.' After a pause he added. 'They're all closed now. Hardly anything uses this part of the river except pleasure boats.'

He broke off and stooped down excitedly.

'Got one!'

'What's that?'

It was a bit of thin white stone about the thickness of a straw and as long as a finger.

'It's what I collect. Know what it is?' He handed it to Roy.

Roy turned it over. Was it stone or was it made? It was smooth, almost slippery. There was a hole running right down the middle but it didn't look worth collecting.

'No idea.'

'It's a pipe stem. The sailors on the ships used to smoke their tobacco in clay pipes. White clay. And they used to break easy – so they'd just throw 'em overboard. They were cheap, see? If you look about you find a lot of stems. And if you're really lucky you'll find a bowl. I've got about twenty bowls, and hundreds of bits of stems. Sometimes you can date them. My grandad had a book which I got when he died and it says when and where they were made.'

Roy began looking around himself, turning over the stones. He picked up bits of glass, and rubbed them, fascinated by the sandy feel and the jagged edges worn to smoothness. White glass, brown glass, green glass. Ringer, though, concentrated on pipes.

'I got one bowl from about 1680. Imagine being in the water all that time. Being covered and uncovered by mud every day for 300 years, until I picked it up. Things keep getting uncovered because of the tides. It's not like on the land where things just get deeper and deeper. Here the mud is always moving.'

They had come to the edge of their bit of beach. Ahead was grey mud. A supermarket trolley stuck out of it, nearby were a couple of road cones and the handle of a wheelbarrow. Ringer led the way up the beach to the made-up bank. It consisted of large stones stuck together with concrete, and sloped upwards for about three metres, the structure just visible under fine green strands of waterweed.

Ringer clambered up and Roy followed. At the top it was dry and Ringer sat down. He took off his backpack and opened it, taking out a plastic bag and a bottle.

'Sandwich?'

Roy took it gratefully.

While he ate, with the other hand, Ringer placed in a row the few lengths of pipe stem he had found. He changed them around until he was satisfied, holding them with great care as if they were fine jewellery.

'I think of a man on a sailing ship. He's got a beard and a woolly hat. And he's on watch. He gets his pipe out and his tobacco pouch. He starts to fill his pipe and the pipe breaks. The sailor swears and throws the pipe overboard. I think though he's got another – so he's all right for a smoke. But each one of these bits was thrown over the side with a swear word. In lots of different languages. Each one could have a label with its swear word on.'

The thought set Ringer laughing. 'Imagine that in a museum!'

Roy put out his bits of glass. The white bits were like little ghosts or patches of mist, the green like bits of soap, and the brown like a dried liquid gum. He rubbed the faint roughness of a white piece, and wondered how the water did this to glass.

'You wouldn't know where these were from,' he said.

'Bottles most likely.'

'What sort of bottles? Beer, wine, soft drinks, food, medicines, chemicals . . .' He struggled for more but couldn't add any to this list.

Ringer shrugged. 'That's why I like pipes. I know exactly what they're from. Grandad . . .' He stopped in a sigh of memory. Roy waited but the words had been quenched by a sudden sadness that came over Ringer. All that moved of him were his fingers, which had decided, it seemed of their own accord, to change the positions of the pipe stems.

'When did he die?'

'Two years ago. Or was it three? I didn't come up here for a while, 'cos it was the place I always used to go with him. I thought I would just be miserable. Then I did come, and it wasn't miserable. I mean he liked it here – so why should it be? I think of the times we walked along together looking for pipes. What he used to tell me. He's got a grave in a cemetery not far from where I live – but I never think of him as being there, in the grave, but out here. I talk to him sometimes. I mean if he was a ghost this'd be where he'd come. I tell him about what's going on at home. Or I show him a pipe bowl I've just found. And I yell – "What d'ja think of this, Grandad!" Sometimes people up there . . .' – Ringer indicated the wall above them where there was a walk – '. . . look down and think I'm crazy. But then,' he mused, 'I think they are. Why walk up there when you can come down here?'

At that thought Ringer bounced up. 'Come on. There's a good bit of beach further up.'

They walked along the top of the bank, past the mud bank below, until they came to a beach of stones and sand. They slipped down the stone defences, which had begun to dry out in the afternoon sun. The green colour of the weed was fading, going a pallid yellow as it dried.

This beach was about a hundred metres long with deep grey mud at either end. It was perhaps thirty metres from the bank down to the water's edge. Ringer immediately began searching for pipes while Roy went down to the edge, and let the waves lap over the feet of his boots. The soupy liquid of the river flashed in the sun. The two ferries, one on either side of the river, were filling up, lorries coming on board. A little later there was a loudspeaker announcement telling drivers to put their handbrakes on and what to do if there was an emergency.

Roy felt a sense of panic. What was he doing here? Why hadn't he gone to the Baths?

He wanted a bike. He meant to get a bike. And yet he was here. He turned and looked at Ringer, who was wandering about in no particular direction, bent over, turning over stones. This place belonged to Ringer.

And he knew why he was here.

If he hadn't come today he would never be asked again. That was clear. Ringer was telling him secret things. This was a place you couldn't take just anyone to. And if they turned you down – well that was them written off. So he'd had to come.

He turned back to the river. On the far side, beyond the jetties and the wall, were blocks of flats, houses, factories. Behind all those windows lots of people, some rich, some poor buying lottery tickets and wanting to be rich. Who was it who said who should have what? Who handed it out? God? Then how did God pick you out? Did he say 'You'll be dressed in rags and live on the streets, and you can have a £300 bike whenever you want one.' Did he choose you by the colour of your eyes or was it just like beans being picked from a jar?

'Got one!' came a yell.

Roy glanced over and saw Ringer with his arm in the air doing a dance on the spot, circling round and round showing his find to the river, to the ferries and to Roy.

'It's a really good one!' he yelled as Roy crossed the stones to him.

When he arrived Ringer handed him his find. Roy took it

gently in his cupped hand; it was a complete pipe bowl with about three centimetres of stem.

'Maybe Sir Walter Raleigh had that one.'

'It's great,' said Roy, meaning it. 'You'd think the tides would break it up.'

'It's been buried in mud. That protects it. It's got the maker's mark on the side. See? I can check that in my book when we get home. It's a brilliant one.'

He hopped about chortling.

'Hey, Grandad! What d'you think? Another one for the collection!'

Roy plumped himself on the pebbles, feeling a little jealous of the love that Ringer had for the ghost who shared his collection. He would like to share something. Or maybe he wouldn't. If you keep it to yourself then no one can laugh at you. No one can think you a fool.

He watched Ringer dancing about, as if there were a secret music coming from the river or oozing up from the beach. He wished he could hear it and dance too. He wished he could find something that would give him that much joy. He took out his glass pieces from his pocket. They were so plain and ordinary compared to the magic that Ringer had found. Just bits of glass worn misty and round by the water's flow.

One by one he threw them into the river.

A little later Ringer joined him and they ate the last of the sandwiches. They washed them down with the water he'd brought. Roy closed his eyes and the sun against his eyelids blazed bright red. Then the question just came out.

'You ever steal anything, Ringer?'

'What's anything?'

'Just anything.'

In the silence Roy watched the particles shifting in the warm redness. Why did he have to ask such a stupid question? Ringer was probably wondering why, and might even come up with a good guess . . .

'A couple of things from shops,' said Ringer. 'Once a little aeroplane still in its bubble pack. And me mum found it. She went wild. "I'm not having you ending up like your dad!" On and on she went, all for a stupid little aeroplane . . .' He was silent a little while then went on, 'She made me take it back to the shop. Can you imagine? This tiny little aeroplane – I'd already taken it out of the wrapping. I had the wrapping in one hand, the plane in the other. I had to say sorry to the shop-keeper, an Indian man. Then he told me off, and Mum paid for the plane. She told Grandad too. He didn't tell me off. Didn't even mention it, but every time I looked at him for about a week I wondered whether he was thinking about it. In the end I wished he'd just told me off like everyone else.'

'Is there anything you'd like to take?'

'What, you mean like the Crown Jewels?'

'No. Something you want. Really want.'

Ringer thought a while, then said, 'If I want it I'll buy it.'

'Suppose you couldn't afford it?'

'You can't have everything.'

'Why not?'

'My dad wanted everything. Look at him. Banged up for the next five years. But he didn't know what he really wanted. Did he?'

'He wanted a lot of money.'

'There was never enough money for my dad. There never could be enough. The amount he spent on booze and gambling and women. There'd be ten of them at a restaurant, big meal, lots of courses – and Dad would pay for them all. It made him feel big. We never used to see him for months. Then he'd come back broke and beat Mum up. And plan another job. 'Cos he was spending it so fast. The money went through his fingers like water. And what's he got now? A prison cell he shares with two other guys. He told me they fight all the time. For two hours a day they get away from each other, for a bit of exercise and a bit of TV – then it's back to arguing about nothing. Every day for years and years. But when he comes out he'll just plan another job . . . until he's back inside where he'll be when he's an old man with sticks.'

The stones were hot under Roy's hands. He scraped the top ones away and found those underneath to be still wet.

'So what you gonna nick?' asked Ringer.

'Me?' he replied, startled.

'Yeh.'

'I wasn't thinking of nicking.'

'So why d'you ask me?'

Roy thought a while. He wanted an answer that would hold Ringer back, that would not let him guess what he wanted to do.

'It was just with your dad,' he said at last, 'I thought . . .'

'I might go the same way?'

'Yeh.'

Ringer shook his head. 'I pay my way. If I want it I save for it. It's why I got the paper round.' His fingers were changing the order of the pipe stems, putting the biggest first. 'Sorry about you getting sacked.'

'Me too.'

'I had a word with Mr Patel. He says no way. I really tried for you. But he never changes his mind.'

'Thanks for having a go.'

'Doesn't mean you can't come to Uncle's.'

'Yeh.'

Though Uncle's was the last place he wanted to be. This trip with Ringer had just delayed things. That's all. First thing tomorrow he'd get the bike. Then take the bolt-cutters back. It was going to happen.

Ringer had gone back to searching for pipes. He was scrabbling through nearby shingle, looking under big stones.

'You're lucky,' Roy called to him.

'Why's that?'

'Cos the things you want don't cost anything.'

Ringer grinned and threw a stone into the river, bouncing it twice. 'And I'll tell you what's luckier.'

'What?'

'Nobody but me wants 'em.'

A little later, foodless and waterless, their faces stretched by the wind and sun, they walked home.

Chapter 16

As he came up the stairs he could hear the piano.

Roy went into the sitting room, where his mother was seated at the piano. He stood at the door for a second, listening. She stopped and turned to him.

'Carry on,' he said.

'I just . . .' She looked a little guilty like she'd been caught doing something she shouldn't.

He said, 'It's the first time I've heard you play in this place.'

She turned back to the piano and began playing again.

It was a piece he'd heard before. Some classical piece. He knew she wasn't playing it very well. Its rhythm was too jerky as she struggled with the harder bits and played the easier sections more smoothly. It seemed more like a fight than a pleasurable thing.

She stopped and closed the music. 'You may not believe it but it's a very nice piece.'

He smiled, unsure what to say.

'You should say, But you played it very nicely, Mother.'

'But you played it very nicely, Mother.'

It was her turn to smile, wryly. 'Not exactly convincing. But it'll have to do.'

She continued trilling on the piano, messing about with some chords. He noted the painting had been finished but, although the windows were wide open, the smell hung in the room. He looked at the carpet, remembering the flood of paint, all the newspaper and water. It was wet, and pale in places where the paint had sunk in.

'I'll get us a rug,' she said, hitting a long note. 'When I can afford it.'

Roy didn't say anything. Not wanting to open it up again.

'Where have you been?' she said.

'Along the river with a friend.'

'I'm glad you've found a friend.' She got up and went to him and kissed him on the forehead. 'Sorry about my temper. It's just been too much for me. The move. All the hassle of it. The money.' She separated from him, wandering around the room. 'And then being here where I don't know anyone. It's all right for you kids – you just walk down the street. And when you go to school you get to know lots of people. But how do I get to know anyone?'

'Not by drinking.'

She shot an angry look at him. 'You think I don't know that?'

'I don't know why you do it,' he said helplessly.

She crossed to him in two strides and held him by the shoulders. 'Because I don't know what else to do.'

He turned away from her scorching eyes.

'How do I start?' she said releasing him. 'All those people out there. How do I start?'

'You just do things,' he said.

'Like what?'

'Well . . . like walk down the road.'

'And then?'

'Find out what's going on.'

She laughed. 'When I was little I had a story book, and in it this little bird went round asking different animals, "Will you be my friend?" And all the different animals – the cow, the horse, the pig, the cat – they all had different reasons for saying No. Except at the end when some or other animal, I can't remember what it was, said to the little bird, "Yes, I will be your friend." But that's how stories go – isn't it? You can't imagine the little bird saying, "Well, as no one will be my friend I will just go out and get hopelessly drunk." The End.'

'No one would buy the book.'

His mother laughed. 'Anyway I'm sober. That's the first battle won. And as you said there isn't any food in the house – that's a good reason for going down the road.'

71

'Sing a song first,' he said.

'All right.' She sat down at the piano, took a music book from a pile at the top and opened it. 'What shall we have? Let's have a look. One we both like.'

'"Jerusalem",' he said.

'My son's got good taste,' she said as she flicked through the book. 'Must be well brought up.'

It was a song he loved the tune of. He didn't understand it all but knew it was about someone who wanted better things. Like he did. Like his mum did.

> And did those feet in ancient time
> Walk upon England's mountains green?
> And was the holy Lamb of God
> On England's pleasant pastures seen?
>
> And did the Countenance Divine
> Shine forth upon our clouded hills?
> And was Jerusalem builded here
> Among these dark, Satanic mills?

And then they walked down the road.

Chapter 17

Roy got up without having set the alarm. He ripped his bike tower off the wall. Eight quid, that was as high as that was going to get. He tore it into strips, deliberately from one end to the other. Then he bundled up the shreds and crushed them in his bin.

He was at the top of the tower now. Well, almost. He checked under his mattress for the bolt-cutters. They were there, in the carrier bag, wrapped in paper. As if half believing they might have disappeared in the night and some scrap iron put in the newspaper, he unwrapped them.

He practised using them. Opening and shutting them. He got a felt tip pen and put it between the jaws. He pressed the handles; the pen snapped in half.

Good.

They would cut anything.

His fingers ran over them. The cold, solid metal, the symmetry, the beautiful design of them. He wished on them as if they were magic.

'Get me a bike,' he whispered.

They could be magic for all he knew. How did things work? Who said what happened when?

'Get me a bike.'

Roy put the bolt-cutters back under the mattress. He was thirsty. Just a quick drink and then he'd go off and do what he had to.

Mum was up and hoovering the stairs.

'I'm glad you're here,' she said. 'I want you to help me put the sitting-room curtains up.'

'Oh, Mum – I've got to go out.'

'This won't take you long.'

'But I need to . . .'

She sighed as she carried the vacuum cleaner to the top of the stairs. 'I can't put them up on my own. If you want them up . . . If you want a sitting room . . . If you want a decent place to live . . .'

It was at this point that Roy realised how early it was. Not even eight-thirty yet. There'd be hardly anyone at the Baths. His plan had always been to have a choice of bikes. So he had time to waste.

'All right, then.'

'Oh thanks, Roy. I just want to spend a few hours getting this place straight today. Put curtains up, empty some of those boxes. Then I'm sure I'll feel so much better.'

His mother went to borrow a ladder.

Roy wished it was all over and done with: the chain cut, the bike taken, and the cutters back at the café. He hated the waiting around; he couldn't think of anything else. It was like waiting for his own execution. The same pictures kept coming up: a row of bikes and him creeping up to them; a snap of a chain and a bike led away; a cry of 'Hey, that's my bike!', a chase . . . with several possible endings – he gets away/ he is caught/ he crashes (and is injured/dies/gets caught).

But people steal bikes all the time. Almost everyone who has had a bike has had a bike stolen. And he had hardly ever heard of anyone being caught for it. Of course that doesn't mean they aren't; just with all the bank robberies and murders it doesn't get any space on the news. He'd never seen a headline BIKE THIEF CAUGHT IN THE ACT!

His mother had bought a local paper. Roy decided to test his theory.

He went through the paper cover to cover (what was Mum up to?) and there wasn't a word about bike crime. Not about bikes being stolen, nor about thieves being chased or being caught, or being up in court or dying in crashes. Not a word! And yet there must be loads of bikes stolen every week in the borough. How many? A hundred wouldn't surprise him.

It's just so common he thought, they don't even bother to write about it.

So all right – a hundred and one this week wouldn't make much difference.

His mother came back with a ladder.

'The woman downstairs didn't have one. But the old next man next door did – and then we got talking. He's lived there for sixty years, you know. Must be nearly eighty. He's a widower. Nice old chap. He's offered me some vegetables when I take the ladder back . . .'

While they were putting the curtain up she mused. 'Maybe that's the way to meet people. Go and ask to borrow things . . . The lady downstairs kept apologising for her broken ladder. She doesn't want to throw it out – it's been in her family since the war. I thought of telling her it looked like it had been in the Blitz.'

The sitting room was a lot better with the curtains up. It looked like they meant to stay.

They then began to put curtains up in the other rooms.

'Best to make good use of the ladder while we've got it,' said his mother. 'Mind you – there'll be no reason to go round if I've done everything.' This thought struck her mid-curtain. She just stopped; Roy could see she had been paralysed by a big thought, standing halfway up the ladder, motionless like a statue in a fountain.

'How many things do you have to borrow,' she mused, 'before you can just pop in for no reason?'

'Doesn't just have to be borrowing,' said Roy.

'What else?'

'You could ask something.'

'What?'

'Where the library is or some sort of shop.'

'That's an idea,' said Mum as she turned it over, still holding the top of the curtain. 'Except who could you ask that of? I mean the woman downstairs – yes. The man next door – OK. But I couldn't go three doors away and ask where the library is.'

Roy admitted she couldn't.

'I need a list of things to borrow that are quite reasonable but that not everyone has. And then I can meet all the neighbours.'

She got off the ladder and dropped the curtain, quite excited. 'Where's my notebook?'

She ran into the sitting room and then came back with a pad and pen. 'This is my meet-the-neighbours plan. What do I want to borrow?' She began to write. 'A hammer . . .'

'What for?'

'I'll think of that later. Anyway when you're moving in you always need a hammer.'

'We've got a hammer.'

She brushed this aside. 'Can't find it.'

She wrote some more. 'Fuse wire, fuses – oh that's good! They'll think of us with no electricity, bound to want to help. A screwdriver – what d'you call those crosshead ones? Phillips.' She snapped her fingers. 'Ginger root!' This pleased her immensely. 'If you ask people for something common like a cup of sugar they think they'll never get it back. But something like ginger root or cardamom . . . then they'll probably tell you their favourite recipes.'

As work seemed to have stopped Roy said, 'Can I go out now?'

His mother waved him away happily. 'Yes, yes. I'll ask to keep the ladder till tomorrow. Finish the curtains then. I want to visit four neighbours today . . . So what to borrow . . .?'

He left her working eagerly on her list.

Chapter 18

The sign by the door said: NO RESPONSIBILITY IS ACCEPTED BY THE MANAGEMENT FOR ITEMS LEFT ON THE PREMISES.

Three bikes were on the stands, just inside the railings at the bottom of the wheelchair ramp. Not a great choice. It might be better if he waited around. It might be worse. Besides he couldn't bear any more waiting.

Glancing around, he wanted it to appear as if he was waiting for someone. He had to do what waiting people did. They looked inside first – didn't they? Yes. If a friend was in there . . . That's what you would do. Or would you just wait outside? They had to come out in the end.

To stop his argument Roy went in. There was a short hallway before the counter and the main vestibule where there were a few tables and slot machines. He poked his head round and searched about the vestibule as if he was looking for someone who had been in the pool. The bolt-cutters were in a plastic carrier bag wrapped in a towel. He wished he'd brought a swimming costume too, to make it look like he intended to go swimming. But it was too late for such niceties. Anyway, why have a costume if you are just waiting? Or a towel for that matter.

He had better start thinking straight.

Roy began reading notices. That's what you did if you were waiting and bored. Women's Aerobics, Fitness for Over Fifties, Bums & Tums (with the same instructor as for Women's Aerobics), Indoor Bowls, Children's Swimming Lessons (Beginners, Intermediate and Advanced), Fitness Suite (for individual workouts) and the Pirates' Cove. The latter puzzled Roy – what was it doing in a swimming pool? But reading

77

further didn't make a lot of sense as he wasn't really reading. The words were just passing by his eyes.

There was a set of photographs of serious-looking men and women: the Manager, the Deputy Manager, the Fitness Instructor, the Head Lifeguard, the Aerobics Coach, the Entertainments Supervisor, the Entertainments Deputy Supervisor . . . There were more, getting down to the lifeguards, but by the time Roy got to these he realised what he was doing. Anything, except what he had come for.

He went outside and leaned against a pillar by the entrance. A girl with crinkly wet hair came out. She smiled at him, he tried to smile back but his face was frozen. Two boys with shoulder bags, chatting about computer games, went in. Then there was a gap.

His gap.

What was he waiting for?

Roy sidled along the fence to where the bikes were. They were just about two metres behind it. Two were mountain bikes, the third was a pretty ancient racing bike. This had a D-lock, the bar as thick as his thumb. Forget that one. The other two were chained up, one chain covered in plastic which might keep the rain off but not bolt-cutters. They were both standard mountain bikes, newish, not great – just fourteen gears (only two chain-wheels). Both had side-pull brakes, which was disappointing.

Roy was breathing heavily as if he'd been on a run, his legs shivery. It was a warmish day but he felt cold about the arms, every sound startled him. He felt everyone was looking at him, able to see the fear steaming off him.

He glanced around.

No one.

Roy clambered over the fence. In two strides he was by the bike stands, where he stood with his back to the street, shielding the carrier bag. His fingers fumbled the towel: he had trouble pulling the cutters out and felt he was showing it to the street.

He went for the middle bike.

Roy got the cutter head under a chain link, then pressed both ends of the handles till his fists met. The chain sliced. So easily it surprised him. There was no going back. He had cut the chain! Up to that point he could have walked away – and they could have said what they liked.

From now on they could have him.

Roy bundled the cutters back in the bag, put it on the handlebars of the bike and tried to prise out the good link from the one he'd cut. But the gap wasn't wide enough and he couldn't twist the link out. For perhaps half a minute he worked to separate the chain.

Oh God, it wasn't going to come!

A panic rose in him. Leave it and go.

Roy stopped working on the links. His fingers were thick and sweaty, his heart pounding, but he had come too far to just run off; he knew what he had to do.

Oh pray no one comes!

He took the carrier bag off the handlebars, trembling so much he could hardly control his hands. Without looking about him – he couldn't do that, it would just panic him – he got the bolt-cutters out of the bag again.

It took him some time to get the head under the link. Centuries. It was if he was wearing mittens. His neck had gone prickly and his throat was dry. Closing his eyes in desperation he pushed the handles together as hard as he could.

He heard a clink of chain. Opening his eyes he saw the two ends. The bike was free.

Thrusting the bolt-cutters into the bag he jerked the bike out of the stand. Forcing himself not to rush, he pushed it along the fence and out onto the street. He then wheeled it along the pavement and turned by the side of the Baths down the side street.

Roy had stolen a bike.

Chapter 19

Around the corner from the Baths, Roy wheeled the bike along the pavement. Wheeled it at walking pace because that's how you wheeled your own bike. You didn't rush it, harum-scarum down the road with your coat tails to the wind. You walked, that is if you didn't ride; you walked it gently, quietly, matter of factly, as if you had a perfect right to. Because it was yours.

Roy looked behind him like a terrified fox wondering where the hounds were. But no one had turned into the street with him. Nor was the woman opposite him even looking his way. Well, she was now, but that was because he was looking at her. He stopped at once and pushed the bike off the kerb between two cars. Taking a deep breath and trying to still his shivering body he looked to the right and the left; he was about to go out when he saw a car approaching. He held back while the car came by, then, looking out again, saw the road was clear.

He turned the bike into the road. He grasped the handlebars, swung his right leg over until the crossbar was between his legs with both feet just touching the ground. He pushed off and at the same time swung his right foot onto the pedal. The bike wiggled chaotically forward, the front wheel twisting this way and that as if trying to escape from the rest of the bike. Roy's feet tangled in the pedals, the bike swung sideways, and then fell in a heap over its rider, who landed with a thump on his backside.

Behind him a car hooted. With a start Roy lifted the bike off himself, and gazed at the car like a rabbit dazzled by headlights. The driver was yelling at him from behind the windscreen. In slow motion Roy raised himself, each step punctuated by the car hooter. Shamefacedly Roy held his eyes down as he wheeled the bike between the parked cars back onto the pavement.

There he stood, hanging onto the bike as if it was a prop to hold him up. He heard the car start, he didn't look up as it passed and a yell came through the open side-window:

'Learn to ride it, you little fool!'

The car swept off. Only when it had gone some way did Roy at last look at it, and only when it had turned near the end did he begin to move again. As if somehow movement proved guilt, or as if, like a startled spider, hoping immobility would leave it unnoticed.

Roy swung himself over the crossbar again, this time remaining on the pavement. Two women were approaching, talking about the length of the school holidays. He let them go; watching their backs until he was unable to hear exactly what the government should do about them, make them shorter, longer or perhaps even abolish them altogether. As the words died away he pushed off and swung a foot on the pedal.

The bike wriggled wildly for a couple of metres, hit a wall and then fell over bringing its rider down knee first. He winced and rubbed it, the bike lying across him as he sat on the pavement, proof positive, if it were needed, that the bike had it in for him.

It had never occurred to him that he wouldn't be able to ride it.

He knew of course that it took time to learn to ride. But he had never thought that that applied to him. Other people had to learn; well, they were different. They weren't naturals. But he would be like a fish emerging from an egg; swimming wasn't something that had to be taught. It was like breathing: you did it. And so with riding for Roy; it was only bad luck he wasn't born with wheels.

He rose. More than his knee was bruised. His pride, his hopes . . . He must get away from here. And quickly.

'You all right?' came a shout from the road.

Roy jerked round. There was the boy – what was his name?

– the one on his three hundred pounds' worth of bike.

'I'm OK,' said Roy wiping the grit off his hands.

The boy lifted his helmet. 'I saw you come off.'

Roy shrugged. 'It happens.'

'Looked like you couldn't ride it.'

'I fell off,' he said angrily. 'OK?'

'Sure, sure.'

'The derailleur got caught in the gear sprocket . . .'

The boy's forehead creased. 'Looks all right,' he said, walking his bike closer, still straddled across it.

'Only happens at speed,' said Roy.

'You didn't have much speed,' said the boy.

'Starting speed!' snapped Roy. 'Don't you know anything? All the effort is on the pedals when you start. The force on the chain from a standing start – well, you know . . .' He was throwing everything in. 'The pull from the chain-wheel to the gear wheel, it can shift the sprockets. And once the derailleur starts to go . . .'

'I sort of get it,' said the boy. 'Something got stuck in something.'

'Yeh,' Roy said with relief.

'Quite a fall you took.'

'I'm OK.'

'You were limping just now.'

Roy wanted to kick the boy's spokes in, but worked hard to control himself.

'Just a bang,' he said. 'Nothing serious.'

'You should get a helmet.'

'I should,' he said.

'You must've spent more than seventy quid.'

'What?'

The boy was leaning over his own handlebars and squeezing the tyres on Roy's bike, feeling the frame. 'You said you just had seventy . . .'

'I managed to get ninety,' said Roy quickly.

'I like the colour. Red and black. Smart.'

'Thanks.'

'Hey!' said the boy snapping his fingers. 'I've got some tools. You can fix it now.' He turned to the small bag at the back of his saddle. He undid the button and pulled out a small plastic pack, which he unwrapped. In it were two spanners, one of them a bone spanner, two tyre leavers, a couple of tyre patches, rubber solution, a screwdriver, and some nuts and bolts. Obviously brand new, obviously unused.

The boy held them out to Roy eagerly. 'You want to fix it?'

'Thanks, but . . .'

'Go on,' said the boy, pressing the tools on Roy. 'Use what you want. Go on.'

'I need to take the bike home,' said Roy. 'I need a hammer. I need a vice.' He handed the boy back the tools. 'Thanks for the offer.'

The boy took back the tools reluctantly and peered at the bike.

'Doesn't look that bad to me. Let me have a ride.'

'It's broken,' insisted Roy.

'Just let me have a try,' said the boy.

'I don't want anyone riding it.'

'Then you should take it back.'

'What?'

'To whoever you got it from.'

Roy's neck had gone all prickly. He just wanted this idiot gone.

'That's why me and my dad never buy second-hand,' said the boy. 'No guarantee.'

Roy glanced down to the corner, wondering whether there was any commotion at the front of the Baths. He started to walk with the bike. The boy cycled along with him.

'Dad got the guarantee on this extended, and added it to the house insurance. Yours got a lock?'

'Yes,' said Roy.

'I don't see it.'

'At home.'

'Not much good there.'

'Shut up!' Roy burst out.

'Keep your hair on.'

'Then don't keep telling me about your flaming dad . . .'

The boy's face went dark. 'I saw you fall off.'

'And who asked you!'

'There's nothing wrong with that bike.'

'Get some specs.'

'You make out you know it all. No tools, no helmet . . . and you can't ride it.'

Then the boy was away, pedalling down the road, showing off with no hands.

'Can't ride a bike!' he yelled.

Roy watched as the boy continued up the road yelling. His arms were outstretched, making the same point as his cry.

Roy shivered. The boy knew.

The boy turned the corner with a final yell – and was gone. But he had seen. Roy's throat was dry, his tongue thick. He must get away from here. He gripped the handlebars and began running with the bike. It was madness to be so close. He turned down a side road, feeling totally exposed. He wanted to cry, he wanted to kick something, somebody. He wanted to scream and shriek. It had gone wrong. He should be riding like the wind, he should be part of the bike, so much so that no one would ever imagine that the bike wasn't his.

He shouldn't be running in panic with a bike that anyone could see should be ridden. It was so unfair. It wasn't his fault he had never learned to ride. It wasn't his fault he had never had a bike to learn on.

It was his mother's; it was his father's. It was the fault of this stupid move to this stupid place. It was everybody's fault. All the people that stopped him, all the people that said no. All the people that watched and waited . . . All the people, all the houses, all the gardens, all the cars. All of the crush of them, all around him.

Out of breath, he stopped by a low wall. He sat down, the

bike leaning helpless against him, and rubbed his throbbing knee. He hated the bike. Why had he ever started the crazy thing! Where in heaven's name was he going to put it? What was he going to say to Mum?

This wasn't the bike to beat the world on. This wasn't the bike to ride away from the pack on, to fight your way up the mountains on. This wasn't the bike to speed down the mountainside into the flags, with the brass band playing and the crowd cheering. This wasn't the bike that made you a hero, that made the world yell your name.

This was the bike to hide away on. This was the bike to bury you. This was the bike you wanted no one to see. This was the bike everyone would want to know how you got. If it was his, really his, then he could learn to ride it. There would be lots of time. But not on one that wasn't his. There would be too many questions. All the time. The whole point had been to ride away, not to wheel a bike to wherever he was going to take it.

The man in the yellow jersey never fell off. He rode on and on, rode up to the sky. He didn't sit on a wall, tired out because he'd been running with a bike.

Running with a bike! How humiliating! How cringing!

For the first time the thought occurred that he should leave it. It was no good to him. Just run off without it. Leave it here on the pavement, let anyone have it. What did it matter as long as he could get away from it. This dreadful bike.

How he wished it had never happened!

And then the next thought. With some luck – and didn't he deserve some now? – he could make it never have happened.

With luck the owner was still swimming.

He would take it back.

Chapter 20

Once the idea had come to him it filled him with urgency. He had to get rid of the bike. He had to clean it all up. Had to get back to where he was. Before. Before this useless lump of metal got attached to him. Stuck to him with a glue far stronger than any you could buy. A glue that glued up your brain, glued up your muscles, glued up your nerves. This useless bit of junk had taken him over. Like an alien creature it had enslaved him. His only hope was to get rid of it, throw it off, and become human again.

Roy turned about and ignoring a throbbing knee, ignoring the eyes of passers-by he high-tailed it back to the Baths. As if being pulled in by a magnet, deep in the bowels of the swimming Baths, Roy was drawn, sucked around corners, across roadways, barely aware of anything except the need to get the bike back. Sucked in by the fervent hope that the boy was still swimming.

In the back of his mind was the problem of the chain he had cut. It wormed its way forward though he tried to smother it with the basic problem of just getting the bike back. Yes – back! And then? And then what? He couldn't just put it in the bike stand unattached. It would get stolen. He would have just made it easy for someone else to do what he had done. Someone who could ride it! Perhaps no one would notice. After all you didn't expect a bike to be standing free in the bike stands. So who would look? Someone like himself would look. Someone who wanted to steal a bike would look.

They always looked.

Was there no way out? If the chain was still lying there, then he might be able to put it back in such a way that it wouldn't be noticed that the chain was broken. Was useless. Perhaps no one would notice that the chain just looped around the frame, and the lock wasn't locking anything as the chain was busted. Might not notice, with the chain running through the wheel, that the bike was unchained. Free for the taking.

Roy stopped. Mid-pavement, the heavy metal pressing against him – was this just more stupidity? Built up on the mountain of stupidity he had already constructed like some vast Lego model. What should he do?

Sweating heavily, breathing hard, his body alive with nervous electricity, like so many mad insects running rampant round his body, he made a decision. It came in like a voice of common-sense amongst the fools shouting at the meeting in his head, stilling them all.

He would not allow the bike to be stolen a second time.

The bike had to get back to the owner. That was the only way out of this mess. The only way forward. The only thing to do. Why bring it back just to give it to a thief?

He would attach the bike as well as he could in the bike stand. Then he would stay and watch. Watch until the bike was taken away by its owner. And only its owner.

So how would he know a thief from the owner?

The owner would make some fuss surely? While the thief would just belt off with the bike. Ride it even. Something like that. Surely? Or would the owner just count his lucky stars he still had the bike and sprint off with it, looking to all the world like a thief!

Oh, heavens above! He had to find a way. A way of getting it back.

Get it back. The voice was clear. It came simple, it came obvious through the cackle, through the soft-headed yelling. Go back in time, over the broken glass minutes, through the cannonade, across the minefield to the safe place called Before. Before he had . . . Before he had taken it. That would be the best. Before he had ever thought of taking it. If only! But thought couldn't be rolled back like a carpet. What was thought was thought.

There would always be part of him that was a thief.

So then there had always to be another part of him that knew better. And the two would do battle for the rest of his life. It was a sickening thought. To have a thief always inside you. To have him waiting, watching for an easy moment, for the sleepy time when the sheriff slept. He must chain him, he must drug him, he must beat him to a pulp. His thief must not win! Ever again.

The red brick of the Baths guided him along its length. The many windows knew. Those on this side might not have watched the act but hadn't the message been passed? They all knew what he was. What he would always be. Their straight and small frames sneered at him.

We won't be fooled!

Just because you can't ride it you brought it back. But suppose you had been able to? Would you be here now? Would you have ridden back here? Or would you have ridden away? We know which and so do you.

Roy turned the corner to the front of the Baths and raced along the fence. In deadly panic to get this over, to get the bike back, he blundered into a voice that cut into his body and soul like a meat cleaver.

'HEY! THAT'S MY BIKE!'

Chapter 21

'What you doing with my bike?'

The boy, fierce and angry, was standing by the bike stands holding in his hands the cut chain. He was bigger than Roy, and the boy's fury immediately halted him.

'So what you doing with it?'

The boy left the bike stands and strode out to take possession. His face was contorted in temper. Roy was afraid of what he might do with the chain that swung in his fist.

'I asked you a question.' He grabbed the bike off Roy. 'What you doing with it?'

Roy had been stung by the situation, the shock of finding the owner already there. He was lost for words. But knew he must find some or he was done for.

'If you think . . .' snarled the boy.

'I . . .' tried Roy.

'What?'

'I . . .'

'You'd better tell me. And now!'

Roy swallowed. 'I saw someone stealing it.'

The boy looked at him in disbelief. 'Oh yeh?'

'I saw him cutting the chain. I chased him.'

'Cutting the chain?'

'With these.' Roy indicated the carrier bag hanging on the handlebars, containing the bolt-cutters.

The boy looked in the bag and took out the bolt-cutters. His hands toured the tool then he glanced back at Roy, searching him, deciding. 'Flaming heck.'

'I saw him,' Roy went on, trying to keep the panic out of his voice. 'He snapped your chain. And then he was off. I shouted after him – but he ran away. With the bike.'

The boy had taken half a step back; he put the bolt-cutters back in the carrier bag. He said, 'How come you caught him then?'

"Cos . . . he fell off. He couldn't ride it.'

'Couldn't ride it?'

'Yeh, he was wheeling it along, then got on it. I was watching him all the time. And he fell off.'

'The kid you saw,' the boy said slowly, 'had stolen a bike he couldn't ride?'

'He tried twice but fell off.'

'I can't believe it. Who'd be such a mug?'

'Big kid. Lanky. Ginger hair and black trainers.'

'And you say he couldn't ride it?'

'Fell off twice. Then saw me and ran off.'

The boy shook his head. 'I don't believe it. This kid who couldn't ride a bike. Admit it – you stole it, didn't you?'

'Would I bring back a bike I stole?'

'You'd have to be a dope . . .'

'So why would I bring it back then?'

The boy threw up his arms. 'How do I know? I just come out the Baths and see all this . . .'

'I should've left it in the road.'

'No, look, mate. Sorry, y'know. I'm not thinking straight. Thanks. Sorry, I didn't believe you – but you know how it is?'

'Yeh,' said Roy with relief.

'Shake.'

They shook hands. Roy tried to keep the tremble out of the handshake. He just wanted to get away. The bike was back and the boy believed him, or just about. He wanted to go now. To be miles from here.

'My dad would have killed me. This was a Christmas and birthday present rolled into one.'

'You need a better chain.'

'Don't I just. Thanks though. If you hadn't have seen him . . . Don't matter how many times he'd have fallen off.'

'Probably going to sell it.'

'Well he'd have to. Sorry I was so narked when I saw you . . . but I came out of the pool and there was just this chain and no bike. Then I saw you – and thought you'd nicked it.'

'The big guy,' Roy managed to say.

'Stupid of me. I mean why would you bring it back? Thanks a million. You don't know what you've done for me. Saved my life. I mean it. You don't know my dad's temper. He'd have beaten me black and blue and stopped my pocket money for ten years.'

'I just saw the guy and . . .'

'Would have been easy enough for you to nick it yourself. When he fell off and ran. What was to stop you?'

'I thought of it. Then thought s'pose I had a bike and someone nicked it.'

'I might've nicked it,' said the boy. 'I mean if I saw someone throw down a bike and run . . . And there was no one about. I'm not saying I would, but I might've.'

'I thought this belongs to someone and I bet they're going crazy,' Roy said earnestly.

'I was. Just the chain and the lock wrapped round the bar. Useless chain. Thanks. I really mean it. You saved my life – I don't know what to say . . . except thanks.'

He put out his hand again. Roy took it and they shook. He wanted to be away, he'd got the bike back. He didn't want the boy's gratitude. He just wanted to be off.

'But I'll have these,' said the boy, taking the bolt-cutters out of the carrier bag. 'Well, he cut my chain. So they're mine by rights.'

Roy's heart sank. They were Uncle's bolt-cutters. He had to get them back to Uncle.

'I'll sell 'em,' said the boy. 'And buy a new chain and lock.'

Roy smiled weakly. He wanted to ask for the bolt-cutters but didn't know how. He couldn't say whose they were without incriminating himself. After all, it was the boy who had had his chain cut and so was taking the bolt-cutters in compensation.

Roy said feebly, 'They're good bolt-cutters.'

'Went through my chain all right. Well, serves him right for leaving them.' He looked at his watch. 'Look at the time. I gotta go now. Promised Mum.'

He gave Roy a slap on the back and hung the carrier bag on the handlebars. He swung his leg over the bike.

'I wouldn't mind those cutters,' said Roy.

The boy screwed up his eyes and gave Roy a look that froze him to the core. All his good work was going for nothing.

'You should sell 'em for a new lock,' Roy said quickly, and gabbled on. 'Get a D-lock. You know? Shaped like a D with thick bars . . . No one'll get through them.'

'Yeh. I will. Anyway, thanks a lot. I'll remember this. See you.'

With practised ease he pushed off and cycled along the pavement. He raised his arm in a wave as he went down the kerb onto the road.

'Tha-a-a-nks!'

Roy watched him down the road. Away he went, merging in the traffic, growing smaller until at last his image was cut off by cars and lorries. Only then did Roy turn away from the road.

The boy had gone and Roy had not stolen his bike.

Just Uncle's bolt-cutters.

Chapter 22

'Hi, Roy.'

Roy hesitated at Ringer's door. He didn't know how to start. He just knew he had to tell him about the bolt-cutters – and get his help.

'I'd like a word. If that's possible.'

Ringer looked him over quizzically then said, 'You'd better come in.'

'Well . . .'

'There's no one in but me and the twins. I'm baby-sitting. And I can't stay out here or they'll kill each other. And I'll get the blame. So . . .' He held the door wide.

Roy came in to the usual council-flat short hallway with rooms coming off it. It had an air-freshener, foody smell with suggestions of smells he'd rather not know about. Ringer led him into the sitting room. There was a large, beat-up sofa at one end against the window, a table by a wall with chairs round it, a TV, cupboards and a scattering of toys on the floor and on top of surfaces.

On the carpet two small boys were fighting.

Ringer pulled them apart. 'Pack it in. We've got a guest. Wayne, Clint – say hello to Roy.'

"Ello.'

"Ello.'

'Hello,' said Roy.

'Wanna play?' said Clint.

'What?'

'Fightin',' said Wayne.

'Leave it out,' said Ringer. 'Me and Roy want to have a talk.' He turned to Roy. 'You've got something to say? Yeh?'

Roy nodded.

'Let's have a game first,' said Clint pulling at Ringer's arm.

'After,' said Ringer.

'Now!' yelled Wayne grabbing his brother's other arm.

'I'll crack your heads together,' shouted Ringer, throwing the two of them off.

The twins were cowed, temporarily.

'Let's go in the kitchen,' said Ringer.

He led, Roy followed. They closed the door on the sullen twins.

'Want some squash?' said Ringer.

'Yeh.'

Roy was sitting on one of the stools at a table with a plastic top. Ringer went to the cupboard and got out a bottle of orange. He poured some in two mugs and then took them to a sink that was piled high with washing-up.

'I'm supposed to wash those before she comes back.' He brought the squash over. 'I can't do anything with them around.'

Roy wondered how he could start. There was so much to be said.

'So you got some trouble,' said Ringer.

'Yeh.'

'Is it your mum?'

'Well, not really.' Roy didn't want to talk about his mum. She had something to do with it, in a vague sort of way. Well, she came into it. But had nothing to do with where he was now.

'Your dad, then?'

Roy shook his head. 'No, it's not family.'

Yelling from the other room started up. The twins were fighting again. There were screams and cries and things going bump.

Ringer rushed out and yelled, 'Shut up or else!'

The fighting stopped and Ringer came back.

'That's them for a minute. What were you saying?'

Roy took a gulp. He couldn't look at his friend and began scratching a bit of cornflakes stuck on the table.

94

'I took a bike,' he said.

'Nicked it?'

He nodded.

Ringer whistled. 'I knew you wanted a bike, but didn't think you wanted one so you'd take it . . .'

'I took it back, though.'

'You nicked a bike – then took it back?' Ringer scratched his head. 'Seems to me then you didn't nick a bike. Or not for long. So I don't see the problem. Or am I missing something?'

'To get the bike . . .' Roy hesitated, chewing his bottom lip. 'Well I had to take something else.'

'What?'

'Uncle's bolt-cutters.'

Ringer drew in a sharp breath and slapped a hand to his head. For a few seconds he didn't speak, staring at some spot in the ceiling, making Roy wish he hadn't come clean.

'You better get 'em back,' said Ringer, returning to earth. 'And quick.'

There was an ear-splitting scream from next door. So urgent that it got Ringer straight to his feet. He charged out of the kitchen and into the sitting room, where one of the twins was crying.

Roy stayed on his stool, exhausted. He was halfway there. He'd told Ringer that he'd stolen a bike, told Ringer he'd given it back. Told him he'd taken the bolt-cutters. But hadn't told him that he didn't have them any more.

Roy went into the sitting room, where Clint was crying. His nose was bleeding and Ringer was trying to stem it with a handkerchief. Wayne was in a corner sucking his thumb; cushions and toys were all over the floor.

'He fights dirty!' cried Clint pitifully, blood dripping down his upper lip.

'Let's get you in the bathroom,' said Ringer.

'He scratches!' cried Clint, swinging a kick in the direction of his brother, as he was led out of the room.

Roy sat on the sofa deflated. What was he to do?

Maybe Uncle would think it was someone else. But too late – he'd told Ringer now. That was as good as telling Uncle.

Or was it?

Water was running in the bathroom. Should he leave? Ringer was busy with the kids. He got up to go. But maybe in a minute they could talk again. Roy started picking up the cushions and putting them back on the sofa . . .

Chapter 23

The room was almost tidy when Ringer's mother returned. She came in with a flurry of energy. Roy was instantly struck by how like Uncle she was. A bit thinner, more hair, but definitely the same face and overall shape including the big hands. Ringer came out of the bathroom with Clint, who had a very clean face. His nose had stopped bleeding.

'Do you want the good news or the bad?' said his mother.

'Let's start with the good,' said Ringer.

'Right. Well your dad's coming out.'

Ringer whistled, the air coming out as if he'd been punched. 'So what's the bad?'

'He's coming out in two weeks.'

'You're kidding.'

'I am not.' Her face was steely.

'How d'you know?'

'He told me. He said he was up before the parole board and they agreed to early release. He was cock-a-hoop.' She sighed and sunk in a chair. 'He asked me why I wasn't too happy. I said I was happy for him . . . but . . .'

'But not for us,' chimed in Ringer.

'Not for us.'

The twins were playing together with some bricks as if their fight had not occurred, piling them up in towers. They were not listening to big people's talk. Ringer's Mum turned to Roy and smiled wearily.

'Sorry to ignore you. You must be Roy. I've heard about you. Sorry I can't be more welcoming. But I've just had a terrible day. Visiting his dad. It wears me out.' She turned to Ringer again. 'I've been thinking about it on the way home. I know what he's going to do – he'll be over here, thinking it's like it was. Moving back in. And I won't have it.'

'We were getting on very well without him,' said Ringer.

'I don't want him moving in. I'm not having him back. That's that.'

'I'm hungry, Mum,' wailed Clint.

'And me!'

'All right, all right.' She held up a hand to them and turned back to Ringer. 'You two can go off out. You're a good boy, Ringer. I know they're terrors.'

Ringer said, 'It was all right. Roy helped me out.'

'Thanks, Roy,' she said.

"S'all right.'

He didn't think he'd done much except tidy a few toys. But at last they'd be able to go out and talk. It'd be good to get away from the kids. He just hoped Ringer would be in the mood to listen after the news he'd just got.

'I want fish fingers, Mum!' yelled Wayne.

'And beans!'

'Go and wash your hands then,' she ordered. She pointed out of the room and snapped her fingers.

'Mu-um!' they pleaded.

'Quicker you wash, quicker I start cooking.'

The twins knew their priorities and rushed from the sitting room fighting each other out the door and along the hallway. Mum closed the door.

Quietly she said, 'We're going to have to do a runner.'

'What?'

'I've been thinking about it all the way home on the train. He'll be round here – and he'll expect to stay. And I am not going through that again. I know him too well. He might fool a parole board but he doesn't fool me. We're going to have to go.'

'Where?'

'Dunno. But we're going. I'll leave him the flat. But we don't come with it.'

'It's not fair, Mum.'

98

"Course it's not fair. Since when was your dad ever fair! Don't say a word to the twins. As far as they know we're off for a few days. The seaside. All right?'

'How long for, Mum?'

She looked at him helplessly. 'How should I know?'

'But all my friends! School? I've got it all sorted.'

'Blame your father,' she said bitterly. 'Now off out, the pair of you. I had a word with Uncle on the way up. He'll give you some tea. But I haven't told him about your dad coming out. So don't mention it – I want to sort some things out first. So off with you – I've some phone calls to make.'

'Shall I take the twins? So you can make the calls . . .'

'No, you've done your stint, Ringer. I'll make 'em some fish fingers . . .'

Chapter 24

'You heard Mum – don't mention it to Uncle.'

Ringer stopped and Roy halted by him. The boys had just turned the corner at the high street.

'He'll find out.'

"Course. But leave it a bit. OK?'

'Yeh.'

'He'd just go on and on. I know he would. And I don't want it. Not while I'm eating.'

'Sure.'

'It's bad enough as it is.'

'Don't you want your dad coming out?'

Ringer gritted his teeth. 'I just don't want to do a runner. I live here. He doesn't. I do! I don't want him mucking it all up.'

'You sure he would?'

'How do I know! Maybe he would, maybe he wouldn't. It's not fair. Whatever happens isn't fair!'

Roy wondered how to make it fair. How to make anything fair. Things happen and you walk into them. Like families with or without money, with or without dads. No one asks you – you just come into it. He wanted to bring up the bolt-cutters again – but Ringer was so full of his dad and his mum's plan to do a runner that he couldn't break in. And here he was walking with Ringer to Uncle's of all places. He couldn't face him. He had to make an excuse.

Roy said, 'I shouldn't have been there.'

'You shouldn't,' said Ringer bitterly. 'It was family.' After a pause he muttered, 'She should've saved it.'

'I won't come to Uncle's.'

'Suit yourself.'

'That way I can't say anything. Can I?'

He had found himself a let-out. He'd split off here, say goodbye . . .

Ringer suddenly swung round and kicked the fence with such vigour that Roy jumped back in fear.

'See what it's already doing!'

The boy punched the metal railing. It was a full swing that intended to give and receive a lot of pain. In the instant of its smash and recoil Ringer cried out. Then doubled up, grasping his knuckle. He had been transformed in a very few seconds from prizefighter to a whimpering dog.

Roy hung back, not knowing what to do. He'd been ready to go, wanted to go. Just be by himself. Looking at the heap of Ringer, he thought that his friend – ex-friend?– didn't want him here either.

'I think I've broken a knuckle.'

Recognising a call for help, Roy said, 'I'll take you to Uncle's.'

Putting an arm round Ringer he eased him up. Ringer unwrapped the hand covering the hurt knuckle. The wound was raw and bleeding, patches of skin hanging off.

'Look at that,' exclaimed Ringer in a half-sob. 'What did I have to do that for?'

"Cos it's not fair,' said Roy. 'That's why.'

With an arm round his shoulder he directed Ringer along the road. Ringer stumbled along, hunched, clutching the bruised knuckle, an occasional sob seeping from him as if the anger and hatred had been sucked out of him in that blow, leaving only what lay beneath.

Roy said, 'It's OK. You'll be all right.'

'If it's broken,' moaned Ringer, 'then maybe we won't do a runner.'

Roy was startled. Had that been in Ringer's mind when he punched the railing? Surely not. To hurt himself so they would know he didn't want to go? Surely not.

They had reached the café. On the door was the closed sign.

"S'all right,' whimpered Ringer.

Roy pushed open the door. Uncle was at the counter wiping

it down. He looked up as they entered and immediately saw Ringer was in trouble.

'What's up?' he exclaimed, coming round.

'Ringer might've broken his knuckle,' said Roy.

'Let's have a look.'

Uncle took the boy's hand and squeezed it gently across the knuckle. Ringer winced.

'Let's get you to casualty. Sit down while I put my coat on.'

Roy sat Ringer on a chair while Uncle went out back.

'Stupid, 'n'I?' sniffed Ringer.

'Yes,' said Roy with the glint of a smile.

'I nearly butted it with my head.'

'You'd have broken the railing.'

'I don't want to do a runner.'

'I hope you don't.'

Uncle returned. He had taken his apron off and was wearing a jacket.

'I'll drive you to hospital. No need for you to come, Roy.'

'Thanks, Roy,' said Ringer. 'Sorry about all the trouble I've been.'

"S'all right.'

Uncle led Ringer to the door. At the door he turned to Roy, 'You didn't borrow my bolt-cutters, did you?'

Roy hesitated, then nodded. 'I did . . . but . . .'

Uncle put a hand up.

'Tell me tomorrow.'

Chapter 25

'Mum?'

The heap wriggled and moaned.

'Mu-um. Please get up.'

Roy had gone home after leaving Uncle and Ringer, and now wanted company. He had had too much of himself.

'What, love?' came the deep-down voice.

He pushed the heap. 'It's all gone wrong today. Everything.'

A head peeped out, tousle-haired, bleary-eyed. 'You too, lamb?'

'Everything,' he said. 'I wish I'd stayed in bed.'

His mother pulled herself out a few more inches. 'Some days,' she said, 'just didn't ought to be.'

'I'm so miserable.'

Mum pulled herself up a little further, and then with great effort to a sitting position. 'Me too, lamb. My great scheme fell to bits.'

And mine – Roy thought but did not say.

'I went out borrowing,' she said. 'Oh, what a failure! My grand idea to break into the social whirl of the neighbourhood . . .' She stopped and wrinkled her nose. 'You know – I don't think there is one.'

'A what?'

'A social whirl. The first place I went to – I asked to borrow a hammer. This woman answered and lent me one, without hardly a word. There was no point borrowing it if we weren't going to say anything. Then I thought I'd better use it when I got back. So I banged in a few nails to hang up some pictures – and the head fell off. I couldn't get it back on. Had to give it back in two pieces. Sorry, I said – and she slammed the door in my face.'

'Poor mum.'

'Not to be daunted – you can't say I didn't try – I went two doors away and asked to borrow some fuse wire. A man answered. Oh, he was as tall as – well, two of you. Well, let's say one and a half. Head in clouds, I had to shout up to him. He looked down on me from his mountain peak and asked me what I wanted it for. The lights have gone, I said. So what do you want, he said – 5 amp, 10 amp, 15 amp? I didn't know. I'll come and look, he said. I tried to stop him, I tried ever so hard, but he insisted. Obviously thinking me a mere woman needing a big man to handle difficult things like electricity. So he came in – and lo and behold! – he turned on a switch and the electrics were all working. What could I say! I just had to lie – and say they must have just come on again. He left thinking I was an absolute idiot, that I couldn't even turn on a switch. It was so humiliating!'

'You saw the old man next door, though.'

'Oh I did. I forgot that. And I went back and he gave me some vegetables. So not a total failure.'

'I'm starving.'

'New potatoes – ooh, I quite fancy those, and broad beans . . . I suppose one out of three isn't so bad.'

'It's brilliant,' he said, 'compared to me. I bungled everything.'

'Well, go and put the kettle on – you can get that right. We'll have those new potatoes. You can help me scrub them . . . Then we'll sing a song or two to cheer you up.'

'You won't manage.'

'Bet me.'

'A bicycle,' he said.

'Have you got one to lose?'

'No.'

'Then you can't bet me.'

'I lost a tool,' he said. 'I borrowed it . . . well, sort of.'

'Without asking?'

He nodded nervously.

'Oh Roy!'

'I meant to give it back. But I lost it.'

'You'll have to pay them back.'

He sighed. Would this day never end?'

'Come on,' she jumped out of bed fully clothed apart from her shoes. 'New potatoes and beans. Let's begin from here. Square one – eat.'

'What about that lost tool?'

'Worry about that tomorrow. Now think buttery new potatoes and soft broad beans . . . Picture them, steaming on a plate.'

She pulled him through into the kitchen, put the kettle on and set him scrubbing potatoes while she played and sang 'Dashing Away with the Smoothing Iron.'

Chapter 26

Roy hesitated under the arch of the doorway and watched the flurry of nails piercing the puddles, and popping the shiny skin on the pavement. He had no raincoat; Mum had an umbrella but it was in a box somewhere.

Besides, umbrellas were sissy.

There was no choice really. He ran out into the rain and splashed down the street. At first he protected himself by hunching over and pulling his collar up, but it was useless and he soon gave up. By the time he reached the newsagent's he was soaked. Mr Patel looked at him wide-eyed.

'You here?'

'I just came to tell you Ringer's got a broken hand and can't do his round.'

The newsagent clapped his hands to his head. 'That's all I need. I got one boy off with pneumonia and now Ringer . . .'

'Let me do it.'

Mr Patel shook his head. 'You can't get up in the morning.'

'I'm here now.'

The newsagent looked at the bundles of papers and looked at Roy. He shook his head. 'I can't do this. I'm a businessman.'

'And I'm here.' Roy had nothing to lose. He was here in the flesh and ready and so were all those newspapers. 'Have you ever had any trouble with me on the rounds?' he added.

'No.'

'So you don't want to lose customers – do you?'

Mr Patel with a huge effort said, 'Do you know the Earlham Clova round?'

'Yes. I did it with Ringer.'

Mr Patel handed over the yellow bag. 'Go – before I change my mind.'

Roy needed no second bidding. Drawing the flap over his satchel to keep the papers dry he went out into the drenched street. His hair splattered as he ran, the water trickled down his face. His shoes squelched; the cold water itched between his toes and sucked the heat from his joints. There was no let-up. It seemed impossible the sky could contain so much.

By the corner a car came too close. A cascade of dirty water washed over him. He yelled at it, shaking a fist until the car turned a corner. He was saturated. Rain that he shook off was replaced instantly. His trousers were dark and shiny, his skin shone, his hair was sleeked back as if greased. There was nothing more the god of rain could throw at him, short of lightning.

He did the round quickly, there being nothing to hang around for. In a while, in spite of the rain, he'd warmed up, and to an extent got accustomed to the discomfort.

Motionless in the driving rain, he waited for the starter gun. This was the time-trial section when riders went off at regular intervals to race against the clock. The first riders had been in luck, the storm hadn't started – but he, the last rider, was catching it in full. As if the storm had been waiting for the man with the yellow jersey . . .

Bang!

He rode into the tunnel of water. There was no one to be seen up ahead in the murk, waves of water washed across his face and trailed behind. The swish of his wheels was like a saw slicing through the road. Jaw tight, head down, legs working like pistons he tore his way into the wind and water, through the barrier of pain . . .

The dream broke, burst like a bubble by the thought of yesterday, by the thought of falling off that bike twice. He squirmed. Imagine getting to his age and not being able to ride a bike. He must learn. Where though? How? Maybe he could get up early, before the paper round and practise then.

On what?

He didn't have a bike – remember? And stealing one was out. So what bike? And how? Buy one? What with? He still had to sort out the bolt-cutters . . . Heck. What would Uncle have to say? Uncle knew he'd taken the bolt-cutters. How much did bolt-cutters cost? He had no idea. Five pounds? Ten pounds? Fifty? Unlikely Uncle would let him off. He was getting further from getting a bike, not closer at all.

When he had finished the round the rain had eased up and was dripping lazily. Blue was appearing in the sky. Roy squelched into the shop and dropped off the satchel. Mr Patel held out a small brown envelope. Roy looked at it puzzled.

'Two pound for today. But if you don't want it . . .?'

He took it.

'Do you want me tomorrow?'

Mr Patel hesitated. At last he said, 'If you're one minute late . . .'

Roy danced out into the rain.

Then he went off to Uncle's.

Coming into the café he was instantly struck by the warmth and light, and then by a secondary wave of sauce and frying smells. The place was full and steamy. Uncle nodded to him as he bustled from kitchen to counter and out to tables. Coats and macs hung from chairs, where men hunched behind newspapers, with big mugs of tea alongside plates of fried food and bread and butter.

Uncle passed by, two plates of food in each hand.

'Go wipe yourself out back.'

Roy went through the kitchen, where eggs popped in the pan, bacon crackled and beans boiled like volcanic mud.

In the back room he found himself a towel and wiped himself down. His clothes were wet but he'd have to live with them. When he returned to the café Ringer was there by the window. He waved a hand in a plaster cast and Roy went to him.

'Broken, then?'

'Yep. I've got to wear this for six weeks. Really itches. I want to scratch and I can't.'

'In future don't hit fences.'

'I'm not thinking of it.'

Uncle brought some tea over. 'Roy – Ringer here. Like his new glove?'

'He needs another one to match,' said Roy.

'Your head do?' said Ringer.

'Enough of that,' said Uncle, moving off.

'Daft,' said Ringer, blowing out his cheeks. 'All 'cos of *him*.' He turned to the window where trails of water snaked down like icebreakers cutting through the pearly surface. He stopped a drip with a finger poking out of the cast. 'Me and Mum talked it over. What we're going to do. She doesn't want to do a runner either. Not if we can help it. So we're going to go and see him today. Mum spun 'em a line and got us a special visit. Family crisis. They're letting us 'cos he's paroled.'

'What you gonna say to him?'

'What we think. He can't just move back like he's been on holiday for a month. Mum's divorced. We got our own lives.'

'And if he doesn't agree?'

'Then we leave town quick.'

'Hope you don't have to,' said Roy, thinking of the time ahead, the empty days without Ringer. 'I hope . . .' He stopped. It didn't matter what he hoped, it wasn't up to him. It was all down to a man in a prison who had robbed a bank with a shotgun, a man he didn't even know. 'It's just,' he tried again, 'not fair . . . you, me . . . I don't have many friends. And just as I get one . . .' The words wouldn't come, the thoughts were tumbling over. 'It's not fair,' he added lamely.

'No,' said Ringer. 'It's not.'

They sat in silence a while. Ringer playing with the drips on the window, Roy munching the fried bread without knowing it was there. He felt a chill of loneliness as if Ringer was no longer sitting there, as if he was in the café alone.

Uncle came over on his way back to the kitchen. 'Roy?'

Roy caught his eye. Uncle's look pierced him like a long pin. He looked away.

'My bolt-cutters, Roy?'

Roy took a breath. This was what he'd been dreading. 'Well, you see . . .' he began.

Uncle cut him off. 'I'm busy now. Come back at 5.30 when

I'm closing. And I want the whole story. OK?'

'OK,' he said, seeing only Uncle's apron and not daring to look up.

Uncle moved off.

'So what'd you do with 'em?' whispered Ringer.

'Well . . .' He looked about; Uncle was in the kitchen tossing eggs. 'I just borrowed them . . . and now . . . well . . .' He hesitated.

'Well what? You can tell me.'

Roy felt itchy round the neck, his mouth had dried out. 'They're lost,' he said.

'Lost?' whispered Ringer, pursing his lips as he looked around at Uncle, who was gathering plates in the kitchen.

The café door swung open.

Ringer's mother poked her head round. 'Come on, Ringer. If we're going to get to your dad today we have to catch the eight-forty-five.'

'Right.' Ringer stood up. 'I gotta go. Tell me later. Hey, fancy coming up the beach tomorrow?'

'Yeh.'

'Great.'

'Come on, Ringer,' said his mother impatiently. 'Sorry, Roy – but we've got a train to catch.'

Roy nodded.

Ringer started towards his mother. As soon as he was close she grabbed him by the arm and pulled him through the door, which clanged shut.

Roy almost grinned. The way mothers can do this to you, no matter who is there. He sank his teeth into the fried bread. Agony postponed. Might as well enjoy the food as he was saved from the awkward questions. This morning at least. But what would he say to Uncle in the evening?

If he'd only asked Uncle first – well, then losing the cutters wouldn't be so bad. But just taking them and then losing them . . . How could he have done such a crazy thing! Looking back on yesterday, on that mad caper – it was as if somebody else had done it all. Someone who looked like him, sounded like him, but wasn't him at all.

But it was him who would have to face Uncle.

Unless . . .

An idea wormed in his brain as he caressed the still warm tea.

Chapter 27

He rounded the corner and didn't dare look. His feet kept moving, his hand crept along the railings. He watched a bus in the distance, held his eyes on it as it moved away, getting smaller, its redness shrinking, until it rounded a bend . . .

It was the same time as yesterday so he knew there must be a chance. He was here after all. It was almost as if the film was being rerun. Except this time he didn't have the bolt-cutters. And this time he wasn't going to steal a bike.

He didn't want to look in the bike racks. He didn't want to see it wasn't there. He didn't want to see that it was. He wanted to be King of the Mountains riding away from the pack, with nothing to think about but the effort of the ride. He wanted one set of thoughts, not all this swinging that way and this, not knowing what he wanted or what he was.

Mum had been up when he had got home from Uncle's. The table was covered in newspaper with a heap of black compost in the centre, like a volcanic mountain. By it, like a great liner in a bay was a green window box. She bustled around, her hands black and streaks on her forehead and cheeks . . . She had been to the neighbour two doors away and borrowed a trowel. She'd been invited back for tea.

He let her talk about the wallflowers she was planting. When she finished she was so pleased with herself she played 'English Country Garden' on the piano, leaving black marks along the keys.

There were four bikes in the rack, and one, Roy saw at once, was the bike he'd stolen yesterday. He knew its thin hard saddle, the patterns on the frame. And he knew by the chain . . . Oh, he knew that chain! It was the same one he had cut twice, the same links, the same lock, but shorter as the boy was making do with the longer of the two halves. His neck and back sweated with the humiliation, the memory of taking it away, of falling off. It was hard to know which was worse. Stealing or falling off?

Falling off hurt more, hurt his pride, bashed his dreams – but then imagine he still had the bike! Imagine he *had* been able to ride it! Where would he have put it? He couldn't have left it in the hall. In his madness he had thought about his room and the bit of roof just below his window . . . But imagine carrying it through the house every day!

He couldn't imagine it. He could imagine it. He itched and writhed with the thought.

How he wanted to walk away!

He sat on the steps by the entrance. He deliberately turned his back on the bike. Restless, he got up and walked to the bus stop. He dawdled back from the bus stop and went as far as the corner. He dared not turn down the side road, knowing that if he did he would not come back. He counted the railings. He counted cars. There was no point counting buses as there was too long between the buses. He tried telling himself a story, not a bike story, not King of the Mountains . . . That wouldn't work here. Not so close to the bike he had fallen off.

He told himself the story of a boy who walked up a mountain. Up the mountain road, and as he got higher it got colder and bleaker. The boy was looking for something. His father, Roy thought, and then decided no – that wouldn't do. A dog, yes, a dog. Everyone said it had come this way, so he walked up and up. Into the wind and sky. Into the cold and rock. Until at the top where it was almost flat he rested on a rock by the side of the road. There was no sign of the dog, the road was empty. No – there in the distance was something. Wavering in the road. A rider.

Roy saw he had his head down and was cycling swiftly. He was helmeted and in racing gear. He wore the yellow jersey of the race leader. Closer came the sound of wheels on the road, of the wind against him. As the rider drew near he held up a hand and gave a grimace of a smile. Then he was past in a streak of wind. Roy watched his back climb the narrowing road. Then he was over the top and gone.

A little while later the pack came, noisy, hunting, savage . . . He stepped back off the road as they swept past in a fury.

Then he was alone.

He stopped the story. He couldn't think what dog it was, or why a dog. He didn't have a dog, had never had a dog, wasn't sure he even wanted a dog . . . Stopped, because he knew the day before yesterday he wouldn't have been walking up the mountain. He would have been the rider in the yellow jersey.

At last the boy came out of the swimming baths.

He saw Roy immediately.

'Hello,' he said. 'What you doing here?'

'Waiting for you,' said Roy gripping the railings tightly.

'Why?'

'I wondered,' said Roy, shifting in his collar. 'I wondered if you wanted to sell the bolt-cutters.'

'I do,' said the boy. 'They're no good to me.'

'How much?'

'My brother says he could get twenty.'

'I can give you ten . . .'

The boy was looking at him, puzzled. Roy tried to hold his stare but it was no good. He had to look away. His knees were shaking.

'You took it, didn't you?' said the boy.

Roy didn't reply, watching the boy's feet by the base of the railings.

'You took my bike. Admit it.'

Roy didn't reply and the boy grabbed him by the collar, lifting up his head so Roy's face was close to his. 'Didn't you?'

Roy nodded.

'Say you took it!'

Thick-tongued he said, 'I took it.'

The boy brought up his fist. 'So why did you bring it back?'

Roy didn't reply.

'Not much of a thief, are you?' The fist didn't look very threatening.

Roy nodded.

The boy laughed disdainfully. 'Just as well.'

Roy half grinned.

'And I thanked you for bringing it back.'

Roy muttered, 'Sorry. It was stupid. But you got it back.'

'Yeh.'

They were silent a while. The boy's fist had dropped but his face had grown watchful and sullen.

'So . . . the bolt-cutters?' said Roy warily.

'Not yours – were they?' said the boy.

'No.'

The boy smirked. 'That'll teach you.'

'Sell them to me.'

'Why should I?'

'Because . . . because I brought your bike back.'

The boy thought a while, then said, 'Twenty quid.'

'I got ten.'

'Twenty.'

'If I give you ten now and ten next week . . .?'

'Show us it.'

Roy took out his crumpled wage packet. He emptied into the boy's palm the note and coins.

'All right,' said the boy as he grabbed the money and thrust it in his pocket. 'And ten next week.'

'Yes,' said Roy. The boy was turning away. Quickly Roy added, 'Can I have them then?'

'You think I'd take 'em swimming?' he sneered.

'No,' said Roy, deflated.

'Anyway, if I gave 'em now, you wouldn't give me the other ten.'

'I would.'

'How do I know that?'

'I brought your bike back, didn't I?'

'And lied like a loon.'

115

'I promise to give you the tenner. Promise.'

'You sure want those cutters.'

'I do.'

The boy stared at him hard. 'You don't deserve this . . . but you'd better come up my house. But I'm warning you – if I don't get that tenner I'm telling my dad, and he'll have the cops on you. OK?'

'OK.' Roy felt relief wash over him. 'Thanks.'

Roy knew he would have to get up the moment the alarm went off; Mr Patel would not give him another chance. If he didn't earn that ten quid . . . it didn't bear thinking about.

Chapter 28

'So what'd your dad say?'

Roy and Ringer were lying on a patch of sand surrounded by stones, the river lapping a few metres away. They wore jeans and T-shirts, and were fanned by a warm wind smelling of mud and drying weed. Ringer's cast was already grubby and covered with scrawls and signatures, including Roy's.

'He cried,' said Ringer. 'Across the table in the visitors' room. All those people there. He said, "I've nowhere else to go."'

Roy gathered up some stones and piled them on his left hand. He didn't look at Ringer as he covered first his fingers then the back of his hand, so his arm seemed to be growing out of the beach like a strange tropical plant.

'Mum said to him, "I can't cope with you. We're divorced. You can see the kids when things are sorted out – but not at my place."' Ringer blew out his cheeks and gave a single shake of his head. 'Then he was bawling. It was terrible. His face was running with tears. I wanted to say – Mum, let him stay a night or two on the sofa.'

'Except it wouldn't be a night or two,' said Roy.

'I just wanted to stop him crying. But my mum can be hard . . . She said, "No – that's the way it is. That's how it has to start, that's how it has to go on." She said her place was *her* place and was going to stay her place. She didn't even want him to visit.'

'Wow!' declared Roy. 'Not even visit.'

'If he tried she'd call the police. She wouldn't let him in.' Ringer shook his head. 'I don't know how she did it. She's a hero.'

'Heroine.'

'He's a bank robber. Ex, anyway. Done for armed robbery with a shotgun. He was bawling like she was his mum. But she said No. No matter what he said. He was thumping the table, a warden had to stop him. He pointed at me and said why'd you have to bring him to see me like this?'

Roy thought of his own dad, an out-of-focus picture, face smoothed out like these bits of glass, walking with two kids with buckets and spades. A woman out of the picture . . .

'He was still crying when we left. Then out in the hall Mum started. They gave her a chair and she wept for about five minutes. "I was horrible," she said. Then we went to prison welfare. She told them he mustn't come back. She left a letter for the Prison Governor. When we got home she went to the police. She told them, "I'm divorced. I don't want him back. You must stop him coming."'

'Do you think he'll come?'

Ringer crossed the fingers on his good hand. 'Dunno. Hope not. We're going to do everything we can to keep him out. We'll call everyone . . .' He stopped. 'If we can. If he lets us. And if we can't – we'll scarper.'

'Where?'

'Anywhere.'

'How can he do it?'

'We're not going unless we have to.' Ringer threw a stone with his left hand. 'We like it here. We got friends. This is where we live. But I can't believe he won't try. When he's drunk one night, one afternoon.' He shook his head again. 'But some good news. Mum told Uncle, and he's going to move in for a few weeks.'

'That's good.'

"Cept he works during the day. But at least he'll be there at nights. Mum reckons if we can hold out for three months then Dad'll give up.'

Talk stopped. Roy couldn't think of anything helpful or hopeful. He had a horrible vision of Ringer's father with a shotgun outside their door, yelling to be let in. Running round the house, smashing windows . . . Crying and throwing bricks. Shooting.

When he looked up Roy saw Ringer strolling about the sand, back hunched, kicking stones, turning one over here and there with his left hand, keeping his plastered hand out of the way. Roy marvelled at the way his friend could deal with things. Ringer didn't panic. He could put things aside without getting desperate.

He wished he could.

With a yell Ringer picked up something. He held it up and danced around shaking it.

'What d'ya think of this one, Grandad? Neat bit of bowl. Eh?'

Roy came over. Ringer handed over the pipe. There was a curve of white clay at the front with a hole in where the stem came in. The stem was about two centimetres long.

"S'a good one,' said Roy, beginning to understand what Ringer was going for.

'I get lucky when you come.'

Roy gave it back and began searching himself. He picked around the stones and saw a rusty, encrusted ring of metal. He picked it up and the brown flaked off on his fingers. He wondered what it had been for, when it had been useful. Roy was about to spin it into the river when he thought this was the sort of thing his mum liked. More junk for the mantelpiece. He laid it with their things to take back.

A call from Ringer brought him over to the thick mud at one end of their beach. There, several metres out, was a wheel, half sunken in the grey porridge. His first feeling was disappointment; the wheel was bent. But on looking closer:

'It's got forks,' exclaimed Roy. 'See?'

'That means there's more than a wheel underneath.'

'How much do you reckon?'

Ringer shrugged. 'Depends how deep the mud is.'

'Do you think we can get it out?'

'Not without going in.'

'I want it,' said Roy, his heart thumping.

'And you won't need bolt-cutters,' said Ringer.

'What did Uncle say?'

'He said thanks for putting them back.'

Roy looked sheepish. 'I sneaked them back this morning when he was out with the customers.'

'You don't have to avoid him.'

Roy nodded, his neck prickly. 'When I took the bike . . . it was stupid. You see – I couldn't ride it. Isn't that a joke? I couldn't ride it.'

'If you haven't got one why should you?'

'So I took it back. What would have happened if I could have ridden it – I don't know. The boy saw me bringing it back. I told him I'd chased the boy who took it. He even thanked me! But then he sussed me when I came to get the bolt-cutters back. Stupid.' Exhausted, Roy threw his head back and gazed into the sky. He felt some relief. Ringer knew most of the story now. That left Uncle – well, he'd leave him for a day or two. Then tell him the lot. He'd like to buy him a present, except he wasn't going to have any money for a while.

Ringer said, 'I bet I could get it.'

In a trice he was stripping off. First his T-shirt, then his shoes and socks. He threw them behind him. He took off his shorts, and stood for a few seconds in just his underpants. He looked about him, along the beach, up the bank.

'Oh what the hell!'

He tore off his pants. And stepped naked, except for the plaster cast, into the mud.

'It's freezing . . .' The mud was like cement. It squelched as he waded into it holding his cast up. Now up to his knees, each step sinking deeper.

'I didn't mean for you . . .' called Roy.

Ringer was pale white in the sunlight except for his calves, which were grey and sploggy when he drew them from the slurping liquid. As he moved forward his body became splashed with spearheads of mud, as if he was being attacked from underneath. Suddenly he sank six inches and toppled forwards in surprise.

'Ooops!'

His hands went into the mud up to his elbows before he could straighten himself. Now they were like lumpy gloves, halfway up his arms. He held up his encrusted plaster cast like a trophy, wiggling his fingers out of its muddy end.

'You're suppose to keep it dry,' exclaimed Roy, feeling responsible.

'Now you tell me,' Ringer cackled, turning away and striding on. He suddenly dropped down again and the mud was round his waist. 'You wouldn't believe how cold it is!'

He was about a metre from the wheel, moving in slowly, like a spoon being pulled through cake mix. His arms were ahead of him, half raised, the mud on them dripping down to his shoulders.

Roy, at the edge, willed his friend on. He wondered how much bike there was. Could it all be there? Or just the front wheel and a broken fork? He imagined it being lifted, the mess of mud dripping from it. He began to strip off. Shoes, socks, T-shirt, jeans. He too stopped at his underpants and looked coyly about. Then at his pal who had grasped the wheel in his good hand.

And took them off.

Ringer was dragging at the wheel grunting, his body and face becoming coated in grey, trying uselessly to keep his plaster from getting splattered.

'It's stuck!'

Roy started in. The feel of it disgusted him. Slimy and thick, it had a dank vegetable smell. He groaned at every step, as the cold slime came all round like an animal crawling up his body.

Then he sank to his waist. For a second he felt as if he was being dragged down by the creature of the slime. He was able to keep his arms out and held them out like a sleepwalker as he pushed on.

Reaching the bike the two of them pulled at the wheel. Roy

thrust one hand deep down in the mud, gripping a bar. So it had a frame.

'One, two, three! Pull!' yelled Ringer.

They pulled.

The bike stayed.

'Again. One, two, three! Pull!'

The bike ripped out of the mud and the boys fell over backwards. The back of Roy's head hit the surface and he sank, blackness and pain running into his eyes, and filth into his mouth. He fought and thrashed, spitting out the disgusting porridge – and at last stood up again. Grimacing and choking, he tried to open his eyes and couldn't. His nose was stuffed with lumpy stuff.

He clawed at his eyes, squeezed his nose. Wiped around his eyes yet again, spitting all the time. He tried again to open his eyes. His eyelashes were stuck; he rubbed at them, and pulled them up with his fingers. In front of him was a creature of mud. It pointed in his direction, mouth open, revealing a red tongue and impossibly white teeth.

'You should see yourself!'

'Just look at you!'

Suddenly Roy saw the bike beginning to sink. He grabbed the wheel and pulled. It came out easily. And with it a frame. He laid it across his shoulder and turned about.

Ringer joined him and they went back stride for stride. Emerging like ghouls from the swamp, mud-covered from head to toe. Breathless they lay on the beach. In a little while Ringer got up and began twisting about and thrashing his arms. Mud flew off as he spun and kicked, looking more human each instant. Until at last, instead of coated, he seemed just painted in mud. Then he ran to the river and rolled in the surf.

When they had got off as much of the mud as they could, they washed the bike. The front wheel was useless. It had obviously been in an accident – but the frame looked fine.

As they dressed Roy discovered his bone spanner and was

able to take off the front wheel. He threw it back into the mud. For a few seconds it stayed on the surface, and then the creature of the deep dragged it down.

They finished the water they had brought, drinking and gargling away the mud they had swallowed. Ringer wiped his plaster with a damp sock. He blew down either end to get out as much trapped mud as he could. They did their best to clean out their noses and ears.

'So what d'you think?' said Ringer.

"S'a good frame.' Roy ran his finger round it, looking at the welds. 'I've got a front wheel in the hall.'

'So you got half a bike.'

Roy grinned. 'Yeh. Just need a back wheel, handlebars, brakes, a chain, chain-wheels . . .'

'Nearly half a bike then.'

'Where can I keep it?'

'Uncle's got a shed in his yard. Got tools too.' Ringer paused. 'Remember to ask properly.'

'Don't worry, I will.'

'You'd better.'

They gathered up their things. Roy hoisted the frame on his shoulder. Both boys had a thin layer of whitish mud on their hair and skin as if they had been wiped with a pastry brush. They crunched up the stones.

'Hey!' said Roy suddenly. 'People dump old bikes. Like this one. Other places . . .'

'We could try the canal. It may not be so muddy.'

That set them laughing and pointing at each other.

'You were the creature from the depths!'

'Frankenstein's little brother!'

The joshing continued as they climbed the steps to the road. The afternoon sun glinted on the badge at the back of the forks . . .

Of Roy's bike.